During the Cold War, ruthless and cynical British operative David Morse is sent to northern Alaska, where he meets Miri Smith who is supposedly researching arctic water systems. As a seasoned agent, David has kidnapped, killed, sabotaged, and even seduced in order to obtain information. He plies his tricks on Miri and what he finds out could change his life — or ruin it. Her secret will twist the couple from 1967 back to 1959 and result in a deadly confrontation as they try to reach for an unimaginable future.

Twisting Time
Copyright © 2021 Luann Lewis
ISBN: 978-1-4874-3337-6
Cover art by Martine Jardin

Published by eXtasy Books Inc.

Look for us online at:
www.eXtasybooks.com or www.devinedestinies.com

TWISTING TIME

BY

LUANN LEWIS

DEDICATION

*With love to my husband, Brian Lewis,
who helps me through everything, my wonderful family,
and to the PMG Ladies, who share my inspiration,
especially Ann, Anna, Beth, Bev, Diane, Janet, Jennifer,
Joan, Jonelle Linda, Marilyn, Melissa, Natasha,
Rebecca, Rhonda, and Susan.*

PART I—EARLY NOVEMBER 1967

CHAPTER ONE: FREEZING AGAIN

Thursday

David boarded the plane at Thule Air Force base, none too pleased to be flying from frozen Greenland straight through to the bitter cold of Elmendorf AFB in Anchorage. Yet being the only available British operative already in the Arctic, he was the obvious choice for the assignment. He had a long journey ahead of him.

At Anchorage, a charter plane awaited to take him to Barrow. From Barrow, he would be traveling by snowmobile, given the weather. At least he didn't have to go via dogsled. He had done that plenty of times, but when snowmobiles became viable in '65, his people had acquired a fair amount of the speedy things. He no longer had to deal with trying to hire sleds and teams every time he was sent to the blasted frigid north.

"Are you comfortable, Mr. Morse?" A young Airman offered him a blanket.

"Thank you, yes." He took the scratchy thing, spreading the short scrap over his long legs. *I could do with a double shot of brandy about now.*

With one hand, he lit a cigarette, and with the other, he opened the folder in his lap. The name David Morse was on the British passport he currently held. Admiral Jensen, his *handler*, figured he might as well keep the same moniker for this next assignment.

Why couldn't he have a mission in the Mediterranean

somewhere? At least his destination was Snow Owl Cabin, which meant it would be well-stocked. Those insane American operatives sometimes used Snow Owl for rest and relaxation. He couldn't imagine who in the world would want to go to Snow Owl for a getaway, damned cold up there. But the supplies they kept year-round would be an advantage for him. There was sure to be plenty of whiskey, some halfway decent canned food, and other semi-luxuries on hand. It could be worse.

His only job would be to dig around a bit, see what caused the odd non-earthquake seismic shudder three days ago and get to the root of some peculiar goings-on. Not much detail appeared in the dossier, other than to say that some sort of life form, possibly human, had appeared from nowhere during the tremor. *Might we have aliens? Doubtful.* He chuckled to himself. The only kind of aliens he had ever encountered were of the hostile Russian type. And why did they choose to come during such cold weather? He was tired of shivering.

He looked toward the blackness outside the window and saw only his reflection, appearing less tired than he actually felt. Small lines trailed from the corners of his eyes, but there was still clarity in his gaze. He was lucky to have his particular shade of blue. With just a glance, he could get a point across, intimidate an aggressor, or soften a woman. As an aside, it helped to make him look less fatigued. The edge of his mouth rose cynically as he peered at himself, then he turned back to his reading. It wasn't long before the engine's calm buzz and the plane's soft motion began to lull him into losing focus. His lids grew too heavy to fight sleep.

Friday

Hours later, he was shaken awake by the same Airman who had provided the blanket. David sat up straight, eyes wide.

"I apologize, Mr. Morse," the Airman said, "but we'll be landing in about forty-five minutes. I thought you might like some breakfast."

"Yes, yes. Thank you." With a stretch, he regained his senses, then stood, bent over, and moved to the center of the plane. In the aisle, he was able to rise to his full 6'2" height. He stretched as best he could, then dragged his hand through the mass of disheveled waves on his head. He'd need a haircut after this, but he'd have to deal with the *rugged* look for now. "Is there someplace I can clean up?"

"Certainly." The Airman pointed him toward the back.

David splashed his face with water. He had seen himself look better, that was for sure. He used the towel to give himself a brusque drying, then tried, once again, to get his hair in order, but his fingers made a poor comb. The hair seemed to go where it wanted. When his stomach started to grumble, he decided his time would be better spent getting some breakfast before they landed.

The journey went smoothly to Elmendorf and onward. Then in Barrow, as expected, a large snowmobile awaited him. He stowed his gear inside a sturdy case that had been temporarily affixed to the seat, which was long enough for a second passenger. The vehicle had some power, and he smiled as the snowmobile flew over the blinding hills.

The pale landscape stretched in front of him, and although he had pulled his hood up tightly, the wind blew stray curls around his forehead and chilled his skin. He paused long enough to tie a woolen scarf across the bottom half of his face to keep his face from freezing as he surged onward. With little patience for travel, he liked the speed the snowmobile offered. Plus, the sooner he got to his destination, the sooner he could make his report and be done with this assignment. Nevertheless, the drive took longer than he would have liked. He reached Snow Owl Cabin just before the afternoon sky was beginning to darken.

Pulling up to the cabin, he noted how gloomy and cold it seemed. It was singularly unwelcoming. The key was exactly where Jensen had told him it would be, but he had to jiggle the lock a bit before it yielded. Once he gained access, he stomped the snow off his boots and beat his fur-gloved hands together. Even with all his covering, the cold was still biting at him. His first job was to get the generator going, second was to build a roaring fire in the huge fireplace. He was looking forward to getting all that done and fixing himself a hot drink with a liberal dose of whiskey and maybe a can of whatever food he could find.

An hour and a half later, he was relaxing in an easy chair. With the generator running and the fireplace blazing, the cold eased out of his bones, and fatigue began to set in. He supposed he should figure out his sleeping arrangement. It wouldn't do him any good to doze off in this chair. He forced himself up and ambled over to the window for a random glance outside. He had to do a double-take. Was that smoke in the distance? Who the hell would be out there in this cold? There wasn't another cabin for miles and no camping this time of year . . . no camping this far north any time of year.

Maybe some of the indigenous people . . . But this far north? Now? He knew he should check it out, it was his job, but . . . He stood there, debating. The idea of suiting up and going back out in the cold was completely unappealing.

No use fighting it. Just go. This was exactly why he was here, to find out what was behind the strange happenings in the area. If anything was ever out of place, it was smoke at night, up here, in this weather.

David banged his fist on the window ledge. He groaned and headed for his boots and coat. "Here we go again." He suited up, then went out to the snowmobile.

4

Although he carried a flashlight with him, the snowmo-bile's headlight guided his way. The going was much slower in the darkness, even though the moon's glow reflecting off the snow gave him a fair amount of vision. He headed for the smoke. As he got closer, he was able to discern a spherical tent. *How could that possibly be warm enough for anyone staying up here, especially overnight?*

There was no disguising the noise of his vehicle, so he didn't even try. He pulled straight up to the tent, and a small figure emerged. A young woman with a coat so thin, he couldn't believe she wasn't shivering in the frigid winds.

"Hello," he called out, the gusts whipping the words off his lips.

The woman waved at him. "Hello," she yelled.

"What are you doing out here?"

"A little research . . . on the water." She shouted to be heard over the roar of the wind.

He nodded. "I have a cabin back there." Moving his chin in the direction of Snow Owl, he continued, "It might keep you warmer." He eyed her accommodations questioningly.

"I'm very comfortable."

"Well, you're more than welcome to join me." He was cu-rious about where she came from and what she was doing. He briefly wondered if she might be the reason he was here.

She paused, looking doubtful, then said, "Okay, I'm sure it will be more convenient than this. I appreciate it."

He got off the snowmobile to help her and was stunned that it took her only minutes to tear down her camp. Her equipment was packed neatly into a kit, which closed and locked automatically. The domed canvas collapsed with one touch, but he didn't see how. Then her gear, her bag, and all the extras stacked conveniently into a cart set on skis, which could easily be towed behind the snowmobile. He had no idea how she had gotten here. She had no vehicle, no snowmobile, no dogsled. Perhaps a helicopter?

CHAPTER TWO: SOUNDS COMPLICATED

David had removed the storage box from the snowmobile's seat, leaving room for the woman to ride behind him. She hung onto his waist as he slowly drove them back to Snow Owl.

He pulled into the shed behind the cabin. The woman disconnected and stored her small cart with the tent off to the side, then easily hoisted her gear to bring inside. He locked up the shed, then led the way into the cabin.

"I've never seen equipment like yours before," he said, "very nice."

"Thank you."

She had a slight accent, but he couldn't place it.

"Where is it manufactured?"

"In Sana Mundi."

He paused for a moment. "Sana Mundi? I'm not quite sure—"

"It's not well known to people here."

"I see." David frowned. "Well, why don't you make yourself comfortable?" He pointed past the kitchen. "There's an extra bedroom in there. I'll try to find us both some blankets."

"Thank you, but I have sleeping gear I can use. It is quite warm." She entered the bedroom and started shuffling through her pack.

He nodded, then went to his room to make sure it was made up for the night. When he was done, he called out to her, "Would you care for a drink?"

She emerged from her room. She had shed her coat and

was wearing a sweater and leggings with bulky socks. She was a good-looking young woman with lavish dark hair that hung straight to her mid-back and thick bangs fringing her forehead. Her body was what he would describe as petite, her movements tight, agile. She was almost muscular, yet padded nicely. If he had to investigate what was going on here, he couldn't think of a more pleasant way to do it.

"Some water would be nice," she said, appearing almost shy.

He grinned. "I was thinking maybe something warmer . . . like whiskey."

"Whiskey?"

"Yes." He raised his eyebrows, lifting the bottle and waving it gently. "Whiskey. Would you like some?"

"Okay."

"By the way, what's your name?"

"Miri."

"Miri?"

She nodded.

"Just . . . Miri? Do you have a last name?"

"Um, yes. Smith."

"Miri Smith." He stretched out the words, rolling them on his tongue. Once he had poured a little whiskey in each glass, he handed her one, then raised his saying, "Well, Miri Smith . . . cheers."

"Cheers." She followed his lead, raising her glass, then she brought it to her lips and sipped. "Oh!" She coughed. "This is alcohol." Her face crumpled. "And it's strong."

David gaped at her response. "It's whiskey. You don't know whiskey?" He chuckled. "It'll keep you warm."

"I guess that's true." She took another sip, "Happy days!" She shook her head. "It feels good." And she laughed a little bit. "It does keep one warm."

"Come, come. Sit down." He waved her over to the couch

and took the easy chair leaning back but giving her his full attention. "Tell me, where are you from?" He kept his voice nonchalant, congenial.

"Oh, around here."

"Barrow?"

"No, not Barrow. How about you?" She sat on the edge of the couch, almost formally, as she sipped her whiskey.

"I'm not from Barrow either." He cleared his throat. "And you're doing research?"

"Yes. I'm a Socio-ecological Hydrologist."

"Sounds complicated." He frowned. "I've heard of Socio-hydrology. I'm not so sure about Socio-ecological Hydrology."

"It expands upon Socio-hydrology to include impact upon ecology."

"I see . . ." He nodded. "And who are you doing this research for?"

"The government."

"Which government?"

"Our government."

"Ours?"

"Yours and mine. The World Government." She sipped her whiskey and peered up at him.

"I see." But he truly didn't. He was mystified.

Once they retired for the night, David waited until he heard a soft snore from Miri's room, then got on the short wave to Jensen. "Do you have any knowledge of Socio-hydrology studies going on up here?

"What-hydrology?"

"Socio-hydrology . . . no, excuse me, Socio-*ecological* Hydrology."

"I've never even heard of that."

"Well, I ran across this woman, all by herself up here. Very mysterious. She has some unusual equipment and claims she is a researcher in Socio-ecological Hydrology." David spoke the words as if they were another language.

"Who does she work for?"

"That's the thing, she won't say. Well, she gave me some story about working for *our government*, the *World Government*. Whatever that means. And she claims her gear was manufactured in a place called Sana Mundi. Does that sound Latin to you? Can you get me some information on this?"

"I'll see what I can do."

"Thanks. I'll check back with you tomorrow and let you know what I find out about her equipment."

Late in the night, he stood outside her door. Confident that she was sleeping soundly, he crept in to get a look at her gear. Much as he tried, he couldn't figure out a way to get into the large kit she had brought with her. It was sealed with no apparent opening. He guessed he would have to wait until morning and see if he could assist with her so-called research. That might give him some insight.

CHAPTER THREE: HAPPY DAYS!

Saturday

M orning came too soon for David. Even though there was a pleasantly long *civil twilight*, the time when the sun was just below the horizon, he wanted to roll over and stay under the warm blankets for at least a week. But he heard a noise coming from the kitchen. It wouldn't do to have the woman exit the cabin without him, so he forced himself up and pulled on a turtleneck and warm slacks. He padded out to the kitchen and watched his new friend holding a can of C-ration biscuits and gravy and gazing at it, seemingly baffled.

"There's a can opener in the left-hand drawer," he called out.

She opened the drawer but still seemed puzzled.

He walked over, pulled the can opener out, and held it up. "This."

She took it from him and tried several different ways to place it on the can.

He watched for a moment, then gently took it back. "Like this." He showed her how to grab the edge of the can then turn the knob.

She watched the can rotate, and her eyes went wide. "Happy days! I've never seen one like that before."

"No?" He frowned but kept his voice light. "What do you use?"

"Automatic. But we don't have many cans."

He raised an eyebrow. "No cans?"

"Not many. Glass is more ecologically sound."

"Glass is breakable. Plastic is safer."

She pulled away, shaking her head violently. "No, not plastic. None of that. Plastic is a killer. It kills the animals, the fish. It causes cancer."

"Those are interesting ideas." He peered at her, then took out a pan and scooped breakfast into it. "And do you know how to light a burner?"

She nodded. "I think so."

"Then how about if we cook this up?"

They ate in silence, and David found himself more and more confused by this strange woman. Certainly, she was not from any place he knew of off-hand. Her speech patterns seemed awkward, peppered with odd phrases, like her use of *happy days*, instead of a typical *oh my*, or *good grief*. And she had strange notions about things, almost mentally disturbed, like her odd reaction to the mention of plastic and her inability to make her way around a kitchen. What woman couldn't fix a good breakfast these days?

And how many women worked in the high sciences? These might be modern times, but the universities didn't have a lot of programs for women hydrologists, even now in 1967, as far as he knew.

Something was definitely different about her. Could she be working for a government off his radar? Had they sent a woman to scope out a vulnerable spot for a nuclear missile base? Which government? It could be any. What a perfect place to put both the United States and the Russian countries in danger. Where was Sana Mundi anyway? What was it?

After breakfast, Miri slipped into her room and soon emerged with her outside clothes on. Again, her coat seemed way too light for the temperatures she'd be facing.

"Is that going to be enough for you?" David nodded toward her jacket.

"Certainly. This is completely insulated fabric, good for temperatures as low as negative forty-five degrees Celsius." She paused for a moment. "That's about fifty degrees below in Fahrenheit."

"Yes, I know," he grimaced. "That thin material? It's that warm?"

"Yes. This type of fabric is used to insulate homes and buildings. It's a derivative of old fashioned *Thinsulate*. Or . . . maybe you wouldn't know *Thinsulate*." She bit her lip and appeared to be considering that. "Think about it as microfibers that trap air molecules, so many air molecules that they become a cushion between you and the cold."

"That doesn't make any sense," he began, then stopped and thought, "Well, it does make sense depending upon—"

She cut him off, "It has seven and a half times the warmth of down." She slung her case over her shoulder. "I have to go get samples. I'd like to come back here afterward, if that's okay with you."

"Of course. But let me accompany you." He set down his coffee mug and headed for the coat rack.

"All right. It'll be nice to have help." Her eyes beamed behind her face covering.

Once outside, they trudged west. "Where are we going?" he asked as they walked. The weather was colder than crisp.

"Over to the water. Like I said, I need to collect samples."

"Of water?"

"Yes." She waved her arm and looked across the dim landscape. "Isn't it beautiful out here? What an amazing sight."

He nodded but urged her on. He didn't want to linger for the view.

It was difficult to carry on a conversation with their mouths covered. David had pulled up his scarf while Miri wore some sort of stretchy material that wrapped around her head like a mask. She strutted along, almost seeming to float over the snow in her lightweight clothes and boots, while he struggled to keep up, weighed down by his heavy fur jacket, thick boots, and big woolen scarf.

David was used to being the lightest one on his feet. He was a fast mover, lithe and strong. Trailing behind another person, particularly a tiny woman, was not something he was used to. Now, he found himself out of breath and panting like a child after his mother. And she scooted along with the large kit bouncing on her shoulder as if it weighed nothing. He was totally befuddled and completely unable to say much, since he was winded.

When they reached the water's edge, Miri somehow unfolded the top of each slim boot so that it rose to cover her legs halfway up her thighs. She stepped forward, opened her kit, and drew out a dipping stick, which she extended further and further until it was quite long. Then she reached out and scooped up water from the depths and poured samples into individual cups. Each cup was carefully sealed, and the lids read *Day 6*.

Once she had about a dozen samples, she put everything back in the kit, closed it tight, slung it back over her shoulder, and turned toward him. "Finished."

She headed back to the cabin with him trailing her once again. Now and then, she'd turn around and point to some particularly lovely — or so she thought. Icy, he thought — view, and he'd nod while continuing to move them back toward warmth.

"I thought you said you needed help," he called out to her.

"I guess I didn't." She glanced back at him, smiling.

He made a face at her, then grinned. "You were playing with me."

She laughed. "What else have you got to do? Drink whiskey?"

It was his turn to laugh.

They got back to the cabin and hustled in the door. "It is cold out there," Miri said, "even in these clothes." She peeled off her coat, gloves, and boots.

"I still don't understand how you don't freeze in those thin garments."

"And I don't understand how you can walk in those." She smiled. "They must weigh seventy pounds." She watched as he hung his jacket on the rack.

"Probably." He smirked.

"Are those from real animals?"

He nodded.

She walked over and felt the fur. "I've read about that. Killing and cutting up beasts for their hides. Strange passion." She pulled back the edge of his jacket and looked inside. "It is quite nice to touch, though."

"You haven't ever heard of a fur coat?"

"We don't have them where I come from."

He frowned. "Where *do* you come from, Miri? I've never heard of a place that has no fur coats and doesn't use plastic or cans."

"It would be very confusing to you, David. I'd rather not talk about it." She turned and headed toward the kitchen. "How about if we make lunch?"

There wasn't much struggle to put the meal together this time. Miri had caught on quickly. Already, she knew how to open cans and how to light the stove. They had a lunch of soup and crackers. Food was limited to mostly C-ration items, but there was plenty of whiskey and cigarettes along with a fair amount of chocolate, which Miri enjoyed. David smoked, but Miri didn't, and she coughed at the cloud wafting around the cabin, so he tried to limit it. That was tough for him, tired and tense as he was.

Their conversation was light the rest of the day, even though David continually attempted to steer it back to her work and origins. Somehow, she adeptly avoided the questions and guided the talk back to him. Of course, he couldn't discuss his work or where he came from, so he gained very little information.

She seemed unaware of anything to do with current movies, television shows, or bestsellers. David held her rapt attention when describing plots and celebrities to her. She also enjoyed his talk about technology and transportation, which he thought a bit odd for a woman. As a matter of fact, when he considered everything, he was surprised at how she had managed to get him to talk so much. It was unnerving, especially when he was usually the one to manipulate conversations.

He had always preferred to steer the chatter in the direction he needed it to take. With over fifteen years of experience at this job, he had his skills down pat. Cocktail parties, quiet dinners, bar stools, whatever it took, he was able to extract necessary pieces of information, often without the other side even realizing they had *spilled the beans*. He wasn't quite sure how he'd slipped up this time. And before he could get a grip on it, Miri was yawning, stretching, and heading for bed.

Later, back in his room, he got out his radio and called Jensen. "Did you find out anything?"

"Nothing. No universities offering Socio-ecological Hydrology, and no women having received degrees in anything close to that. Also, I found no country called Sana Mundi. Still trying to find out if there's a town or village with that name. In Latin, by the way, Sana Mundi means *heal the world*. Good catch on the Latin."

"Anything about a *World Government*?"

"Nope."

"Water research up here?"

"Nothing."

"I don't get it." David shook his head. "All she did today

15

was just take water sample after water sample, and that was it" — he paused — "at least as far as I could tell. But maybe that was a cover . . . for something else. I just don't know what." He narrowed his eyes and stroked his chin.

"Look, Morse, you've got to find out what's going on with her."

"Well, she's not exactly forthcoming with her agenda."

"Remember Belgium . . . Lithuania . . . Madagascar?"

David hesitated, closed his eyes, and murmured, "Yes."

"Try that approach."

"Yeah, sure . . . whatever it takes." He sighed. "I hate that."

"Oh yeah, it's so tough," Jensen mocked. "I wish I had it that tough."

David ground his teeth. "I'll get you the information, but it's not as easy as you think."

"Right. Seducing women is such a hardship," Jensen snorted. "I wish I had your looks. I'd be using the Belgium Method on every mission."

"That's because you're the lowest type of human possible," David growled.

"And you aren't?" Jensen fired back. "Tell me again, how many ships you have sabotaged? Planes you've blown up? Ow, I can just feel the pain up there as they ejected." Jensen's undisguised sarcasm dug at David. "Oh yes, and how many kills have you chalked up . . . those guys who were slinking around undiscovered, cooking up plans to have a go at our side?"

David bit back at him. "It's my job, and I'm damn good at it."

"Yes, you are. And how many women have you escorted straight from the bed to the prison? Or worse, left behind to deal with the consequence of some double-cross?"

"I don't like that part, Jensen. I never have."

"Yeah, you get lucky, Morse, and you complain. You don't

have to worry about an excuse to escape those feminine clutches in the morning."

David was speechless.

"And you got lucky with the weather this time, too."

"In what way?"

"There's a huge storm heading toward Snow Owl."

"When?"

"Tomorrow afternoon. You two should be locked in that cabin for a couple of days—nice and cozy."

"Okay."

"You've got enough supplies, right?"

"Yeah, but it's not exactly gourmet eating up here."

"You'll have to find something else to occupy yourselves." Jensen snickered. "In the meantime, we've got a team on the way up there. We'll take the girl into custody for further questioning, but we're not moving in until you're finished with her."

"Got it, Jensen. Over and out."

"Out"

CHAPTER FOUR: DO YOU ALWAYS WAKE UP LIKE THAT?

Sunday

David startled awake at the feel of a light tap on his shoulder. He leapt from his bed and pushed the intruder up against the dresser, pistol to her head.

Miri's eyes were wide. "Happy days, David! Do you always wake up like that?"

"No." He shook the sleep from his head. "No." Putting the gun down, he said, "I apologize. I sometimes get . . . a little tense." He tilted his chin down and rubbed his forehead.

Miri reached out and gently touched his arm. "It's okay. I wasn't afraid."

He narrowed his eyes at her. Was she comforting him? Her hand was on his arm. Most women would be shrinking away, hysterical. Then he noted some sort of fragrant aroma coming from the kitchen.

"Miri, did you make breakfast?"

She nodded and smiled.

She had mixed up some powdered eggs, added salt, pepper, and some dried spices along with a few crushed crackers, creating a sort of goulash that was remarkably tasty. He said as much to her, and she blushed.

"Do you cook at home?"

She nodded. "I enjoy it, but my kitchen is not like this one."

"No? What is yours like."

"Well," long pause, "the appliances are a bit more modern." She snickered.

He gazed around, "I suppose any appliances these days are a bit more modern."

After breakfast, she went to her room while he finished cleaning the dishes. She emerged wearing her outdoor gear and let him know it was time for her to collect her samples.

"How do you manage to fit all your equipment into that one kit?" he asked.

"It was specially made for this project."

He walked over and inspected it, running his hands up and down the edges. "How does it open?"

"Only to my fingerprints."

He looked up at her, startled. "Really? Why so secretive?"

"Not secretive . . . efficient." She shrugged it off. "Are you going to join me again, or is it too much for you?"

David could tell she was laughing at him. He smiled at the mischievous light in her eyes. And as much as he hated wandering around in the cold, he had a job to do. It was time to turn on the charm. "I wouldn't miss it for the world."

He slid into his heavy fur jacket, wrapped his scarf around his neck, and pulled the gloves on. Following behind her, just as he had done yesterday, he struggled to keep up as they headed for the water. Once again, she collected sample after sample, only this time the lids on the little cups were labeled *Day 7*. When she was done, they went back to the cabin.

The afternoon lay ahead of them. After warming up by the fireplace, David offered Miri another whiskey, and she accepted. She still shuddered a bit with her first few sips, but she was apparently beginning to enjoy it.

"Happy days, you'll have me addicted to this drink by the time I return home." She stretched and leaned back on the couch. "That won't be good, because where I come from, people don't drink it much."

"Well, they drink it a lot here." He chuckled, scooting a bit closer to her on the couch. "What shall we do this afternoon?"

"Hmm." She returned his smile. "How about a game? A competition?"

"A competition?" This surprised him.

"Sure." She tapped a finger against her lips and gazed upward. She picked up a pad of paper from the coffee table, ripped a piece off, and crumpled it into a ball, then made a second one. "We'll put these, one for each of us, on the floor, then get on our knees and blow it from one side of the room to the other. Let's see who can do it the fastest." She was visibly excited by the idea.

"You want me to get on my knees and blow a piece of paper?" David was incredulous. He had never had such a suggestion made to him by a woman — or anybody — before.

"Sure, it'll be fun." She slapped him on the thigh, then moved to the other side of the room and got into position. "Come on."

He felt embarrassed, idiotic, but what choice did he have? He was trying to loosen her up, make her a friend. *Okay, on my knees, with a ball of paper.* He picked up his wad and walked across the room to join her. Down he went, all six feet two inches of his frame, long legs crunched. This was not particularly comfortable.

"Pull ... Release ... Pop!" Miri called, then leaned down and started blowing on the ball.

"Whatever happened to *ready, set, go?*" he complained as he followed her lead. He awkwardly bent down to blow on the ball as he looked forward and saw her attractive figure poised, end up, in front of him. At least the view was good. He smiled. He didn't care if he lost, which was surely going to happen.

When she got to the other wall, she turned around, face flushed and laughing. She looked at him and said, "Happy days! You're going to have to move faster than that. Don't you know how to blow?"

"No." He laughed. "I haven't been doing a lot of blowing lately." He leaned up against the wall, a bit winded. He sat shoulder to shoulder with her. "This was a ridiculous idea."

"It was fun."

"You have a strange idea of fun."

"What's *your* idea of fun?"

He turned and looked into her eyes, then reached out and pushed the hair from her face. "Something a little more . . . grown up."

She blushed. "I don't know if I'm old enough for that."

He frowned. "How old are you?"

"Twenty-four."

"You're a woman."

She blushed again. "I am?"

He nodded.

"They don't treat me like a woman . . . where I come from. I'm an assistant. Sort of like an intern here."

"Well, you are a woman. A beautiful woman."

Miri trembled a little. "You're not really a woman until you're thirty or so."

"Thirty?" He was more confused than ever. "Some would consider that old."

"Old?" she squeaked. "Happy days, that's just beginning."

"Miri." David scowled. "You have got to tell me where you're from." He got serious. "What are you really doing here? I need to know."

She rose to her feet. "You wouldn't understand. It's nothing bad." She walked toward the kitchen. "I'll be leaving in a few days anyway."

Chapter Five: Would You Like to See My Body?

David followed Miri into the kitchen. "I need you to open up your gear for me," he said with a stern voice.

She shook her head. "My research is too important. I can't have you tampering with it." Looking down, she continued, "I'm sorry."

"So am I." He headed toward her bedroom, walking through the door with her following. He grabbed the kit and began to pry at it.

"You can't get into it."

"Oh, yes I can." He walked over, grabbed Miri by the wrist, and held her hand in the air. "You'll open it for me."

They struggled for a moment as he tried to force her over to the box, intending to place her fingertips on it. But she suddenly pulled against him, and before he realized what was happening, she shifted her weight, yanked him against her thigh, and flipped him to the floor.

"I'm sorry, David, but I can't let you examine my research." She actually did look sorry.

David pulled himself up and dusted himself off. "I wasn't quite prepared for that."

He walked toward her, and they began to tussle again. She was good and fought hard. She got him to the ground twice, and he did the same to her. She was agile and found his vulnerabilities quickly. He was strong, though, and almost as quick as her, but his size actually worked against him.

On the other hand, he was simply more muscular and eventually had her pinned against the wall. "You *are* going to open the case," he said through gritted teeth. "Simple as that."

Suddenly he heard a clicking noise and felt a zap of electricity. He fell to the ground and couldn't move a muscle. It took a minute or two before he could move again, his head spinning.

"What *was* that?" he muttered.

"A mini-taze . . ." she answered. "It's much safer than the old fashioned tasers of your time." She frowned. "Or, I guess you don't have tasers yet. That's not until the seventies."

"What are you talking about?" He couldn't think straight, could barely even get up.

"It's a small protective weapon." She helped him to his feet and to the couch. "Please don't try to get into my things. I don't even know why you would try."

It felt good when she brushed the hair off his forehead, then she brought him a glass of whiskey.

"I guess you like this stuff." She knelt in front of him and looked into his eyes. "Are you feeling better?"

He nodded. "Yes, much. Thank you." He shook his head gently, still feeling dizzy. "Miri, I honestly don't understand who you are or where you're from, but you're making me believe in aliens, mystical creatures, all sorts of things. What is going on?"

"I'm really not supposed to be interacting with anyone here," Miri said. "I should have never come to your cabin . . . but I was curious."

"Miri, this may be the ranting of a crazy man, but I've got to ask you something . . ."

She lowered her chin and looked into his eyes. "Yes?'

"Are you from . . . from some time in the future?"

She sighed. "Yes."

"When?"

She didn't respond for a while, looking doubtful. "I'm not sure I should tell you."

"You can't *not* tell me now. I keep secrets well. Besides" — he grimaced — "do you think anybody would believe me if I told them?"

She smiled. "I'm from the year 2165."

A sense of awe swept over him. "2165? Nice to know the human race makes it until then."

She smiled. "I'm glad you know. It's been hard sitting in here with you, not being able to be myself. You're so different than the men in my time. It makes me feel odd, stilted sort of."

"What are the men like in your time?"

"They're all kind of bigger than you . . . not taller, but like bulgy, I guess. You're very sleek, like a cat. Your body is interesting. The men in my time are more like gorilla people." She laughed.

He laughed, too. "Is that a compliment?"

She nodded.

"What about the women?"

"We're more . . . well . . . muscled . . . than your women."

"I noticed."

"Is it ugly? Are we gorilla women?"

"Not at all."

"Do you want to see my body? To compare?"

"See your body?"

"Yes. You know . . . how I'm built. Nakedness is not a shame, at least in my time. I know it's embarrassing in yours."

"Uh . . . this is a bit awkward. Of course, I'd like to see your body, but not the way you mean." He was caught off guard. "In these days . . . these times . . . uh, now . . ." He cleared his throat. "We see each other's bodies when we care about each other . . . when we want to touch each other."

"It's that way for us too, but we can also look at each other without having to touch. It's natural curiosity."

24

"What else is different in your time?" He steered to another subject. "Do you still have cars?"

"Sort of. We have vehicles that coast above predetermined roadways, and we punch in our destinations. It's safe, and there are very few accidents. There are no injuries or fatalities at all. Sometimes a computer error causes a minor collision."

"Miri, you have a million pieces of information to share."

She shook her head. "I've told you too much already. That's all I can say. I was instructed, specifically, not to share anything with anybody. If I encountered anyone, I was only to protect myself. You see, I can twist time if I tell too much. I can twist time with just the wrong words." She looked worried. "I can twist time if I don't return when I'm supposed to. I can twist my own future, my own body. If a woman doesn't return when she's supposed to, she can become infertile. Or if she already has children, those children can become sick or even disintegrate."

"Do you have children?"

"Oh no, I've never even been married."

"They still have marriage in 2165?"

Miri laughed, "Of course. People still partner—men and women, women and women, men and men, or sometimes more than two."

"What?" David couldn't help his incredulous gasp.

"Yeah, some of that will start in your time." She laughed.

He shook his head. "It's a stigma now. That's hard to believe."

"You'll see. But, again, I've said too much."

They continued to talk, but she skirted his questions about the future. He felt better after a while, and they made themselves dinner. Neither of them noticed the storm setting in until the noise of the wind whipped around the cabin. It roared so loudly that it grabbed their attention away from their conversation.

"It sounds bad out there."
"Yes, it does."

CHAPTER SIX: SONG OF SOLOMON

David walked over to the window and pulled the small curtain back. Miri joined him, and they both looked out into a white nothing. The blizzard obliterated their entire view.

"I hope it stops by tomorrow," Miri commented. "I have to get out there again for day eight."

"How many more days?"

"Three."

"What is it all for?"

She bit her lip. "I suppose I can tell you that." They moved over to the couch. "In the coming years, small particles of plastic make it into the deepest parts of the oceans. The material embedded in the life down there ends up causing a great deal of harm. We are trying to determine exactly when it all began and the stages of damage during different generations in history so we can send remediation to the period that would be most effective in resolving the past and thus affecting the future." She looked serious. "And, yes, that's twisting time . . . but we're hoping to twist it in a positive way."

David felt a little overwhelmed by all she described. "So, that's why the fear of plastics?"

"It's not a fear. It's an abhorrence."

He nodded. "I think I need another whiskey."

"Me too." She got up and refilled both their glasses. "I'm getting used to this drink."

He chuckled and raised his glass, "Cheers."

"Cheers." She laughed. "That's an interesting toast . . . but a happy one."

They sipped their whiskey in momentary silence.

"I really like the way this feels." She stretched as she sat, leaning against the back of the couch.

David admired her curves. So feminine for someone who could sling him to the floor. Now, though, he had to find out if there was more to this whole thing than what she was telling him. It was all well and good to hear that she was from a different time . . . if that was even true. Still, if she was, could she be doing research on water only — or was she researching something different? Something to do with turning their governments into what she called the *World Government*? It sounded communistic to him, which was something he needed to investigate.

He relaxed, took a sip, and smiled contentedly. "Isn't this better than blowing paper across the floor?" He kept his voice friendly, and his eyes partially closed.

She chuckled. "In a way . . . but don't think I'm letting you just do drinking. I thought of some other games, and we're going to play them. I've still got three more days." She raised her eyebrows and poked his leg.

"You're bad," he growled, then reached out and refilled their glasses. Unfair, he knew, but he needed to loosen Miri's inhibitions . . . and her tongue.

"I'm going to get intoxicated," she objected, her voice indicating that she was well on her way. Still, she continued sipping. "Does it always feel this good?"

"Always." He leaned toward her. Her hair smelled clean and a little like winter chestnuts.

On the one hand, he didn't feel right about approaching her this way, but on the other, it was pleasant. It was easy to bury his lips in her cool dark tresses. He heard her take a deep breath. *Good, she likes it.* He trailed kisses lightly down the side of her face, stopping at her ear to let his breath linger. He felt the effect he was having on her and enjoyed the way her body softened and how the pulse in her neck sped up.

She pulled away slightly and gazed up at him. "You have such a beautiful face," her voice was almost a whisper.

"Me?"

She nodded and ran her finger up the side of his cheek. "Complex bone and muscle structure."

He grinned. "I guess that's a compliment."

"And your eyes. It's like they have their own light." She cocked her head to the side and looked into his eyes as if he were part of her water samples. "Amazing."

"I feel like I'm under a microscope." He cleared his throat.

"His legs are as pillars of marble, set upon sockets of fine gold," she began in a gentle voice. *"His countenance is as Lebanon, excellent as the cedars."* She dragged a finger across his lips. *"His mouth is most sweet: yea, he is altogether lovely."* She smiled up at him.

"Sounds familiar." He frowned, trying to think.

"Song of Solomon. King James Version. Describes you perfectly." She turned to her whiskey and took another sip. "Not so much microscope. More like awe. You're like the man in Song of Solomon."

David was surprised to feel himself blush. He didn't think he'd done that in about twenty years. He, too, turned to his whiskey glass, but instead of a sip, he took a big gulp. "So, they still have the Bible in 2165?"

"Of course. They have all the religious writings. You can learn about them in school or just take the ones you're interested in."

"So people still have religions? Religious beliefs?"

"Yes, we respect all religious beliefs, and of course, we have the World Belief, too."

"Which is?" His curiosity piqued.

"We will put others' interests ahead of our own."

29

"And how is that carried out?" He raised an eyebrow.

"We abide by the World Rules. All children are exposed to the rules from the time they are born. When they enter school, they are taught the rules, first and foremost. Of course, they also see them lived out at home and in their neighborhoods."

"What are the World Rules?" He sat up and faced her. This was getting interesting.

"They come from philosophies built by generations before us, from a time when people spoke them but did not live them." She paused for a moment, then began her recitation. "No one may kill except the government. We will not harm anyone physically, emotionally, or materially. We will seek first to listen and then to be heard. We will seek first to understand and then to be understood. We will seek first to love and then to be loved. And to do that, we will share our joys, sorrows, anger, and forgiveness." She nodded. "Those are the core ways to live that every child learns."

"What happens if somebody breaks those rules?"

"They are gently reminded of them. Most people realize they have not put others' interests first and ask forgiveness. Of course, they are always met with grace."

"What if they refuse to ask forgiveness and continue to break the rules?"

"Well, that mostly happens in school, when children are still learning, but sometimes it happens with adults. Then they are strangled-out."

"What in the world is that?"

"There is a mask that goes over their head and covers their mouth tightly so that they cannot speak." Miri raised her hands to demonstrate. "It winds around their neck so that if they move to hurt someone, it will tighten on their neck, then it is tied to the wall or a chair. Their hands are bound and their feet, also. They must sit in the chair until they are ready to ask forgiveness or even just to comply with the rules."

"That sounds horrendous." David pulled away from her. "And the other kids gawk and make fun of them?"

Her eyes widened. "Of course not. How terrible! No, the other children each give that child a piece of candy or a special gift from their desk. To remind that child that he, or she, but it's usually a boy" — she smiled — "are loved and already forgiven even before forgiveness is asked. At the end of the day, the child gets to take his bowl of gifts and candy home no matter the outcome."

"It seems like a kid might *want* to get strangled-out just so he could get candy and gifts every day."

"They could, but no one seems to want to."

"What about adults?"

"They get strangled-out, too."

"In public?"

"Yes."

"With gifts?"

"Yes."

"Does it work?"

"Often."

"And when it doesn't?"

"The government has a place for those who don't comply, and if they must, they have leave to euthanize them, but that hasn't happened in decades."

David nodded, looking into his glass. "What if you don't like rules?"

"There are some who don't like rules. Some who live behind the mountains. Sometimes they even want to fight us."

"I think I'd be like that. I don't like rules. I'd be more of a freedom fighter."

"A freedom fighter?"

"Yes." He lifted his chin and gazed directly into her eyes. "I like freedom."

She looked puzzled and tilted her head. "And from which

rule would you want freedom?"

He thought for a moment.

"Would you want freedom from putting others first? Or from listening before being heard or seeking to understand before being understood? Or would you want freedom from loving before being loved?"

"Well . . ." he huffed. "Sometimes there are things that must be heard first before listening . . . Also, I prefer to make sure that I do the hurting before someone hurts me. That's how I stay alive."

She nodded, "Yes, our little ones are like that. The three- and four-year-olds pull on their mother's arms and don't like to wait or listen. I suppose I can understand your resistance to listening first. They want their way and react without thinking."

He looked at her to see if she was teasing him, but her expression was serious.

"And I suppose you must hurt others," she continued. "You're a product of your time, and your people haven't learned to receive pain without retaliating."

"Pain without retaliating?"

"You're brash." She spoke with tenderness. "You wanted to see my equipment, so you tried to force me. You believe in freedom and would fight for it, yet you pulled me by the hand, hoping to take my freedom from me." She smiled and drew her finger across his brow. "You're like our little ones, and your face is like a little one's, too. The way you hold your mouth, your lips are almost like a pout. But your brow, it's like a scowl. It does something to my insides. It makes me lose my breath."

CHAPTER SEVEN: THE BELGIUM METHOD

As Miri stroked his forehead with her cool fingers, David felt his heated intensity and tension melt away. He collapsed into the feeling and leaned his head against her chest. *This is not a good thing.* Yet it felt so pacifying. She was soft, inviting, and caressed him like a cherished child.

She leaned forward and kissed his head. Little darts of excitement ran through him. He wanted to lie back and have her kiss him all over while he stretched out and felt her hair drift across his naked skin. He tried to shake that thought from his mind but could only bury himself further into her, kissing her breasts through her sweater while she held him.

"You're so starved," she whispered. "Your heart seems to ache."

She was right. He *was* starved, but he'd never let his desires interfere with his work.

"And so sweet," she murmured.

If he hadn't been absolutely relaxed, he would have laughed. Nobody had ever called him sweet. He was known for being tough, cynical, or, with women, perhaps suave . . . but sweet? He didn't think his mother had even ever called him *sweet.*

But he couldn't laugh. He could barely move—he was completely at ease. He felt drugged. Had Miri given him something, some new sedative from her time? No, she hadn't. He knew that. He just couldn't help but allow himself this moment. A brief respite of forgetting it all and enjoying the feel of somebody who appeared to care. He breathed a long sigh and snuggled more fully into her embrace. He hoped she was comfortable, that he wasn't crushing her. Those were his last thoughts as he fell asleep.

When he woke up sometime later, the fire was merely smoldering embers, and the room had gotten colder. Miri was sound asleep, sitting up and holding him in her arms with her head leaning back and to the side. David rose carefully, trying not to wake her, then gently laid her down on the couch and tucked a blanket around her. She snuggled under it in her sleep. Her cheeks were rosy, and her eyelids fluttered a bit, then she settled into deeper breathing, her hair gleaming in the sparse light of the room. His hands ached to touch her, but he had to get in the other room and check in with Jensen.

He opened and closed his fists a few times, then took a deep breath. *Get a grip, David. You've got work to do.*

He headed to his room and got on the radio with Jensen.

Jensen wasted no time. "What have you discovered about the girl?"

"She says she's from the future."

"The future?" The incredulous tone of Jensen's voice couldn't be missed.

"The year 2165."

"Of course. Well, I've got the team on the way. We'll get to the bottom of it."

"It may be true, Jensen."

"What?"

"I'm serious."

"Really?"

"Yes, she uses equipment that's advanced, claims knowledge of things I've never heard of, and answers questions as if she has experience. It may very well be the truth." He paused. "There are just some concerns I'm trying to address."

"Okay. But she'll have to be debriefed. There is an immense amount of information we'd be able to extract from her if she is truly from the future."

"Most assuredly. You'd be amazed at the technology she possesses . . . even has a simple small weapon."

"A weapon, you say?" He sounded startled.

"Just a small one, for personal protection, apparently. But, if our operatives had access to these things, it could be lifesaving."

"I'm looking forward to talking with this girl."

"So, when will you be here?"

"Our team could be to Barrow in a day, but that storm is sitting right over you, and we won't be able to get there until it lets up. We'll be stuck in Fairbanks or close to it."

"Okay. Well, I'll keep seeing what I can get out of her until then."

"Good job." He paused. "Are you using the Belgium Method?"

David growled. "Yes, and I don't like it."

"Why? Is she ugly?" Jensen chuckled.

"Not like that, Jensen," he snapped. "It's just dirty work, that's all."

"Seems pretty pleasant to me. If I could get the girls, I'd be more than happy to do it."

David scoffed. "That's because you have no conscience."

"Since when did *you* get one?"

"I'm out."

Jensen laughed. "Out."

David slammed the microphone back on the radio, then shoved it back into the wall. He looked over his shoulder to make sure he hadn't awakened Miri. He was half afraid she'd be standing there and he'd be forced to own up to what he was doing out in the middle of nowhere.

The wind outside was whipping up, groaning and howling

like a wolf in pain, and the air in the cabin had become bitter cold. He figured he should get the fire going again and stop worrying about everything. Jensen was right—he had a job to do, and maybe Miri *was* actually plotting something. All the rhetoric about grace and forgiveness could have been designed to put him at ease. It certainly worked.

His head was spinning. He had to remain focused on getting information from Miri . . . solid information . . . not philosophical ideas from the future.

Chapter Eight: The Storm

Monday

David sat in a chair opposite the couch, sipping a cup of coffee as he watched Miri wake up. She stretched in such a way that made him want to run his hands over her lithe body. But that was not going to happen unless he needed to . . . for information. And only for that reason.

"Breakfast?" he asked.

She nodded with a sleepy smile. As she rose off the couch, David noticed she had shed her sweater and leggings at some point during the night and now wore only a thin set of long underwear.

She walked to the window, rubbing her arms, then looked outside. "Oh no, it's still storming. I can't see anything." She turned back to him, frowning.

He had a hard time keeping his focus on her face. She had dimples in certain places that were clearly noticeable through the delicate material. He almost lost his resolve, wishing they could both get under the blanket and . . .

He cleared his throat. "What's wrong?" *There . . . much more down-to-business.* It wasn't like him to give in to distraction.

"I've got to get to the water." She appeared agitated, pacing back and forth, all muscles and flesh. "How am I going to do this?"

"Miri, could you go put some clothes on?" His voice cracked, so he cleared his throat again and peered into his cup, stirring vigorously.

She looked down and frowned, seemingly unaware of how sheer her coverings were. "Okay."

A few minutes later, she emerged from her room in a tight sweater and leggings that outlined every bit of her body. David decided to pour himself a whiskey.

"Whiskey for breakfast?"

"I need it."

She gave him a puzzled look. "Is everything okay?"

He nodded.

"David, I've got to get to the water again. What am I going to do?" She sounded frantic.

"Stay a few extra days." He shrugged. "Get the samples after the storm blows over."

"You know I can't do that."

He frowned. "Why not?"

"I told you before. If women stay on the wrong side too long, they can become infertile." Her voice rose, slightly shrill. "I haven't had children yet. I don't want to time-twist my own body." She went to the window. "But I really need those samples."

He followed her and looked out. "We don't have enough rope to get to the water."

"You need rope?"

"Yes, in the old days, farmers used to string a rope from their homes to their barns to find their way back and forth. The blizzards were so bad they could actually get lost on their own property. They'd die out there, frozen to death midway or wandering, unable to find their home just yards away from them."

"That's horrible."

He nodded.

She snapped her fingers. "David, I have some line . . . perpetuline. It's small and clear, but it's unbreakable. I have lots of it, all on spindles. There's surely enough to make it to the water. You could hold it at this end while I go get the samples." Her eyes lit up.

"Oh no," he shook his head. "I'm not letting you go out there alone."

"How will we—"

He held up his hand. "We'll anchor it here. We can do that safely on a nail . . . or several nails." He thought for a moment. "How many spindles of this perpetuline do you have?"

"Two."

"Okay, we'll use both. That way we'll have a backup in case anything happens."

After a quick but hardy breakfast, David prepared to execute his plan and sent Miri to get the spindles from her kit. The spools were compact, and he marveled at their construction. The thin yarn-like line was pliable and easy to work with, yet try as he might, he could not break it. He couldn't even cut through it except with a tool Miri supplied.

Once he got the spindles solidly anchored to the cabin, he tied the line from one spindle to himself and the line from the other spindle to Miri.

David dreaded the arduous walk ahead of them. Miri's gear was light, as always, but even carrying no equipment, the walk would be nearly impossible due to the shifting snow mounds. He dug out a couple pairs of beat-up snowshoes and poles, which would make the trek a little easier. Finally, he used his thick rope to tie Miri to him, realizing that with her petite size and lightweight gear, the fury of the storm could sweep her away, while his coat and boots would keep him more anchored. They each donned protection for their faces and pulled their goggles down, then stepped out the door.

The winds immediately buffeted them with blisteringly icy gusts. In spite of Miri's confidence in her clothes, David could feel her shivering. Suddenly, just as he had predicted, the wind picked her up, and she had to cling to him to keep from flying backward.

He held tightly to her hand as they fought against the force of the storm in order to move forward. *All this for a couple cups of water.* He grimaced. But if she wasn't lying, it could be a couple cups that might help save the future. *Hah, how could that be? This has to be a pile of rubbish. Whoever heard of such a thing? Plastics. Why am I out here, anyway?*

Still, he forged ahead, putting one foot in front of the other and dragging her behind him. He wasn't sure he had ever done anything quite so grueling. Every few steps, he tested the perpetuline to make sure it was still holding. All was good.

After what seemed like hours, they reached what he believed was the water's edge. He signaled to Miri, and she fell to her knees and opened her kit with shaking hands. It was obviously hell for her to get her things together to take the samples. He tried to position himself to help block the wind, but the gusts came crazily from side to side, up and down, throwing her off balance and whipping her supplies around. Eventually, she managed to use some strange device to burn a hole in the ice and collect her samples until she got enough water that wasn't blown away. Once the last cup had been sealed, she closed the kit and stumbled to her feet. He felt her shivering so convulsively that he became concerned about her even making it back to the cabin.

He grabbed her, parted his coat slightly, then pulled her into it, holding her close to him. So much cold emanated from her body that he wrapped the fur more tightly around them both and held her. He tucked his head next to hers and stood there, sharing his warmth until he thought she'd be able to make the walk back. She slid out from his arms, and he began the trudge, using the perpetuline to guide them through the blinding white.

He was stunned to find that not one trace of their walk to the water remained. If they hadn't used the perpetuline, they would have been lost forever, wandering in this horror. He contemplated the explorers of old and those who must have died hiking these areas long ago. Thinking of the fire and heat awaiting them back at the cabin, he quickened his steps, and they made it to the door, in good time, exhausted and bright red from the icy winds.

They were chilled to the bone and ravenous when they entered the cabin kitchen. David grabbed a couple of cans of beans and opened them. It didn't matter to either of them that the food wasn't heated, they were starved. They wolfed it down and drank several shots of whiskey, then made their way to the fireplace.

David stoked the flames higher and huddled with Miri under a blanket. His cheeks and fingertips went from tingling to burning, but he ignored it, since it felt too good not to be cold. After a few minutes, they finally regained enough energy to talk.

"I may have to go back with just eight days' worth of samples." Miri sounded dejected.

He nodded.

"That was truly horrible."

"It was," he agreed. He turned to her with a smirk. "I thought your jacket was good up to fifty degrees below."

She looked up at him and smiled. "Yes, I thought so, too." She shivered. "They lied."

"Maybe it was colder than that."

"Maybe."

CHAPTER NINE: LIKE ATLANTIS

They drank a little more in silence, both still completely fatigued. Finally, David pulled back from the fire and leaned against the sofa. "Miri, tell me more . . . more about your world."

"Well," she said and leaned back next to him, "what can I tell you that won't twist up time?" She closed her eyes and tilted her chin. "Our kitchens are better than yours. I've seen mock-ups of your kitchens in museums."

"Really?"

"Yes, your . . . your ranges." She pronounced the word as if it was from a foreign language. "We don't have ranges. We have wavemounts."

"Wavemounts?"

"Yes, sort of like microwaves but faster, safer."

"Microwaves? People use microwaves in their kitchens—regularly?"

"Sure, I think that started back in your time . . . maybe. They were invented back in the Bronze Age."

"The Bronze Age?" He chuckled

She laughed. "Just a saying. They were really invented in the forties or something."

"I know when they were invented. In 1945, following the invention of the cavity-magnetron by a Brit."

"I didn't know that." Her eyes widened.

"See? You don't know everything." He laughed and bumped her shoulder with his. "So, other than your kitchens, what else is different about your world?" He cocked his head.

"What exactly is the *World Government*?"

"It's our government," she answered. "The way we govern ourselves. Honestly, it can get a little boring."

"What about countries?"

"Oh, we still have countries."

"Who governs them?"

"They follow the World Government system."

"What kind of system is that, exactly? Presidents? Armies? Congresses? How is it structured? How do you protect yourselves from others?"

"The World Government protects us when needed, but it rarely is. In our town, we have a council who makes sure the infrastructure is kept up to date, but there's nothing much to it." Miri bit her lip. "I think one of the reasons I was sent here instead of a more thoroughly educated researcher is that I have a very limited field of knowledge. They picked me because I focused on ecological science all my life, not history or political science. They wanted to make sure I couldn't twist anything up. I was a very good choice for this work."

"So, are children only allowed one track of study? Education isn't broad?"

"Well, it's as broad as you wish it to be, but I was only interested in this area. Some people, like me, are born with the kind of brain that focuses on one thing. In your day, people didn't understand that and gave labels, saying those children had disabilities. In my day, we're allowed to pursue our passion and not forced to waste time on other things."

David mulled that over. "Like a savant, you mean."

"Well, kind of like that." But she frowned and shook her head. "For me, from the time I was a child, I was drawn to nature and our impact upon the natural world." She shifted to turn toward him, eyes lighting up. "Do you know that entire pieces of land have been submerged simply because the glaciers have melted?"

43

He just stared at her.

"Not yet, of course . . . not in your time. But by the time your generation gets finished with the earth, there will be melting, causing water levels to rise. Indigenous tribes will lose entire cultures, and small cities will sink. Not unlike the tale of Atlantis . . . except it will be real." She nodded. "It's true."

"Because of plastics?"

"Oh no, not just because of plastics. That's only part of it, but I couldn't even begin to explain it all to you. Our whole mission is to eventually place people back into the appropriate times and places to make a difference without, of course, twisting time."

"And if you twist time?"

"That is not my specialty." She shook her head. "But I now know more about it than I might have, because they sent me here. It would be destructive . . . very destructive. First for the person who twisted it, then it could cause much larger shock waves. Who knows?" She raised her palms. "Our scientists have to figure out exactly how to go back and make tiny tweaks, enough to change the ecological course of the world without harming the general timeline." She took a sip of her whiskey. "My small part in all that is to bring back samples so that they can check the amount of plastic already instilled into your water systems."

"And what else are you doing here?" He leaned into her. His slight scowl seemed to go unnoticed.

She laughed and shrugged, "That's all I can tell you except about mundane daily life. Ecology is my passion." She smiled up at him. "Ecology and dogs. I have a dog."

"What's his name?" David took a drink and leaned back.

"Her name."

"Her name." He smiled.

"Terra. T-e-r-r-a."

He snorted. "Figures. Roman Mythology . . . Terra Mater?"

"Yes," she chuckled. "Mother Earth. You're well-read. But I just call her Terra for short."

"Well, here's to Terra." He lifted his whiskey glass.

She clinked hers against his. "You know, I'm going to miss this drink when I go back."

He gazed down at her. "Is that all you're going to miss?"

She looked back up at him. Firelight shone in her eyes. "No," her voice came out a whisper. "I'm so scared."

"Of what?" He frowned and turned his head to see her face more clearly.

"That nobody in my time will make me feel the same excitement that you make me feel, here, in your time."

Chapter Ten: First Time

David stared at Miri for a moment, feeling a flicker in his chest, not unlike the snap of the flames coming from the fireplace. He set his glass down, then took hers and put it to the side as well. When she reached for him, he trailed kisses down her neck. He knew what to do, knew how to make a woman react. He was a pro at this. Yet with her, it felt rather wrong. Perhaps because she was from a different time — if she really was. He had to remind himself that nothing was proven yet.

Finally, he brought his lips to hers and teased her, pulling away then pushing back. He almost smiled when her mouth chased his in a little dance of desire. Then he pulled her closer and deepened the kiss, his tongue tangling with hers, and she responded with small moans, melting against his body. They kissed for what felt to be an exceedingly lengthy but pleasurable amount of time as he stroked her back lightly, then slowly dragged his finger down her thigh. She shivered and did the same to him.

When he felt the moment was right, he lifted her sweater slightly and ran his fingers along her exposed flesh. She yielded eagerly, encouraging him enough to tug the top up over her head. He frowned when he attempted to unclasp her bra, a job he ordinarily had no problem executing, except hers had some sort of fastener he had never tackled. She giggled as she undid the closure with one hand. When she slid it off, he smiled. Her breasts were as toned as the rest of her body, yet soft and pliable. He buried his face in the supple silkiness

46

of her bust, then nuzzled each side with kisses, listening to her sounds as he nibbled and licked. He took his time, plying all the tricks he knew to bring her pleasure.

She, in turn, pulled at his shirt and slid it over his head. Then she lowered her hand below his waist and began to rub him gently until he was uncomfortably hard beneath the thick cloth of his slacks. She fumbled at his belt as they continued to kiss. He finally stood and pulled her up, and they both quickly shed their remaining clothes.

He held her away from him by the shoulders. His gaze traveled down her body from her breasts to her waist, hips, and legs. "This is how we look at each other's bodies in 1967, and by god, you're beautiful."

"You are, too." Her gaze roamed over every part of him, then she reached out and touched his chest.

He let her hands roam freely as she circled him, peering at his body as though he were a display. He felt oddly embarrassed as he wrestled with emotions he wasn't used to—a combination of excitement and . . . well, bashfulness, he supposed. He wasn't used to being *examined* by women. He was more used to being the *examiner*. How was Miri judging him? He had his share of scars. Would that disgust her?

She drew a fingernail across his rear and up his back. "You're like a statue from the museum. Just look at you," she murmured. Her fingers felt like whispers along his spine, leaving goosebumps in their wake.

When she faced him again, her lips met his. He ached to touch her and to have her keep touching him. He stretched a blanket out in front of the fire for them to lie down on and began to explore her body. There were so many parts to caress, handle, and stroke. Her little moans, gasps, and long breaths echoed around the room, blending with the sounds of the crackling fire. His hands traveled over her smooth flesh, and he forgot this was supposed to be part of his job. Instead, it was pure pleasure. She was lovely, smart, curious, and adventurous, and when she wrapped herself around him, he grew anxious to be inside her. He reached between her legs and found her wet and ready. As he slowly slid into her welcoming heat, he was met with some resistance and a small gasp.

"Miri?" He pulled back, eyes wide. "You're not a . . . a virgin? This isn't your first time, is it?"

She nodded.

David stopped cold and rolled onto his back, away from her.

"What?" She scooted over to him, then pulled herself onto his chest, looking at him with a hurt frown. "You don't want me? You don't want me because I'm a virgin?"

He looked up at the ceiling. "Your first time shouldn't be like this."

"Like what?"

"Like whiskey . . . and me." His thoughts turned dark, judging his actions.

"I want it to be you." She reached down and touched his vulnerable erection. "I know about this, and I could have had other people . . . many times . . ." Her fingers teased. "But I want it to be you."

He tried to pull away, but she pressed his shoulders gently down and began to kiss his chest, traveling down his stomach. He was weak, unable to move.

"I've read about it. I think I can make it nice. I know what to do. This . . ." Miri whispered and kissed lower and lower down his body, then took him in her mouth.

He felt powerless — with her hands and mouth on his most tender parts — and disgusted with himself. He reached down and half-heartedly tried to push her away, but she persisted. He gave up, moaned, and grasped her cool smooth hair in his fists. Her ministrations became more insistent until he finally stretched to pull her up and crushed his mouth against hers. He touched her secret places, letting his fingers move and probe and circle until she arched her back and cried out, shuddering, shrinking, pushing against his hand. He kept going, supporting her body as she writhed.

Finally, he laid her back and gently parted her legs. "This might hurt for a moment," he whispered and positioned himself.

She simply nodded, eyes wide, as he entered. Her hips rose to meet his, then the dance began and her eyes closed as they clung to each other. All thoughts of right and wrong were driven from his mind except for this moment, this feeling. He felt their hearts beat as one as they tangled chest to chest, their hair mingling on their foreheads, clinging through their sweat, their arms entwined, and her legs wrapped around his.

She held strong as he pulled himself up to a kneeling position, sinking more deeply inside her. Her head fell back with a gasp of pleasure. He smiled at her uninhibited responses as he laid kisses all over her neck. He was going to make her first time a most memorable experience.

He slowed his thrusts, then sped up and slowed again, driving her to reactions he had never seen in another woman. Finally he was unable to hold back. The peak of his passion tore from his middle, then all through his body, his heart, and his mind. It felt unlike anything he'd ever known, almost like a frenzy of ecstasy. It just kept going and going until he collapsed on top of her, wet with sweat and exhausted.

They lay there, breath echoing in the air until he had the strength to roll to the side.

Finally she turned toward him and whispered, "Is it always like that?"

"No, not always," he whispered back and grinned.

Chapter Eleven: Under His Skin

David wrapped his body around Miri, and they slept in front of the fire, curled together, arms and legs entwined as if they were one. Occasionally, he awoke in the middle of the night to adjust a tingling limb and look down at her. She slept soundly, innocently, mouth slightly open, cheeks flushed from their earlier escapades. He brushed his lips against her skin, enjoying the silkiness.

This is ridiculous, unprofessional. Don't get involved. David breathed in Miri's scent, buried his face in her hair, and intensified his grasp on her, feeling protective. He experienced a surge of something that seemed to flow into his chest . . . something he wasn't familiar with . . . something he'd never felt before. Well, maybe back in high school when he'd dated Becky Sanders before she broke his heart.

He was a man of intellect, strategy, not a man of emotions. Every interaction he had with women was carefully planned and thought through. Every smile and wink was simply part of a process, not a true expression of anything deeper. He always had a job to do, and he had always done it. He had intended to do that this time, just as he had a number of times before. Sure, he didn't feel great about having to use these methods, but he would use any technique necessary. He always had. He had killed, sabotaged, cheated, stolen, misdirected, and — yes — seduced in order to thwart *the bad guys*, but that was his profession. He did whatever was required to *save the world*. It was just that some tasks were more distasteful than others.

This certainly wasn't the first time he had been called upon to mislead a woman while in pursuit of information. He had done this with women who were even more beautiful than Miri. But previous women never had this kind of impact on his emotions. Being with them had just been another task, almost mundane. He had been all grins and soft words on the outside while maintaining a solid wall on the inside.

Perhaps this time it was the ambiance here in the cabin, the snow, the isolation. That must be it. This was different. And David had certainly never given anyone their first sexual experience before. He had to admit, he didn't feel particularly good about that circumstance. He would have rather she had that encounter with somebody a little more sincere. Nevertheless, he had gleaned a great deal of information from her.

He broke off his thoughts and glanced down again. Miri was unique. And so trusting. How in the world could they send such a naive and unprepared young girl to a different time? If that was even really true. But if it wasn't true, how could any government send somebody so ill-prepared to do any kind of secretive work? She lay there completely relaxed, completely open to him, not a tense muscle in her body. She knew nothing about betrayal or defenses. He smiled. Sure, she could fight like a beast, but if one gentleman putting on a pretense could get past her common sense, she was, in actuality, totally and utterly unable to take care of herself. He leaned down and kissed the side of her forehead, and the flutter in his chest disturbed his conscience again. *Stop it.*

He slid gently away from her, crept into the bedroom, and pulled out his radio.

"Jensen," he kept his voice low.

"Go," Jensen's voice crackled through.

David quickly turned down the volume. "Have you found out anything further at your end?"

"Nothing. We've hit a brick wall." Jensen sounded baffled.

51

"I'm making headway."

"Good for you. But Morse . . ."

"Yes."

"Weather is still pretty bad there. I'm afraid we're no closer to getting to you and the girl. You'll have to keep holding out."

"I can do that, but you'd better get here soon."

"Why? What's the matter? Is she on to you?"

"No . . . no . . . It's just . . . it's . . ." He bit his lip. "It's . . . getting under my skin."

"Under your skin?"

"I need a vacation."

"You'll get one, Morse, I promise, after this mission is over."

"Good."

"Keep on her, get whatever you can out of her, and we'll take her into custody when we get there, okay?"

"Yeah."

"Out."

"Out."

David pushed the radio back into its hiding place in the wall and sat silently for a while. He lit a cigarette and gazed at nothing. Something bothered him, but he refused to think about what that might be. He stubbed out the butt viciously, then went back to the living room and snuck under the blanket with Miri. He had a job to do, dammit, and he was going to do it. *Get information and stop acting like a schoolboy.*

Tuesday

She was toweling her hair and shivering naked as she came out from showering in the bathroom.

"Come here. You look cold." David held his arms out, and she eagerly came to him.

He pulled her over by the fire, then unbuttoned his shirt

and wrapped it around her, trying to warm her with his body heat. When she kept shivering, he stood, took off his clothes, and grabbed his big fur coat. He sat against the couch and pulled her down between his legs, her back to his chest. He surrounded her with his body then enveloped them both with his coat. Only their legs stuck out, and those were warmed by the fire. He wrapped his arms in front of her and tucked his face close to the side of her head. He felt relaxed and comfortable, leaning back and enjoying the tenderness of her back against his chest. Her breasts rested against his arms, and he moved his hands so his thumbs could stroke her gently. He was rewarded with a sigh. This was exactly what he wanted . . . for so many reasons.

"Warmer?" He whispered.

"Mm-hmm."

He slid his hand down her belly to the apex of her thighs, and her hips rose to meet his touch.

"You're ready for more?" he asked, raising his eyebrows in mock surprise. Then he began kissing the back of her neck and down her shoulders. She gasped when his fingers found her secret spot.

"You make me feel . . ." she murmured.

"Feel what?" he whispered.

"Like I've never felt before . . . like whiskey in my veins." With a moan, she turned to face him, her chest to his, her lips grazing his face.

Her kisses were sweet and gentle, tiny touches all over his cheeks, forehead, jaw, little whispers in his ear . . . Oh, it felt good. He let his head drop back so she could work her magic on his neck. He shouldn't relax, shouldn't be enjoying this so much . . . He should be working *his* magic on *her*, not the other way around, yet he couldn't help but enjoy her delightful attention. He drew in a long breath and let it out in a sigh.

"Is this good?" she asked, wide-eyed.

"Oh, very good." He almost roughly pulled her head back by her hair and gazed into her eyes, silent for a moment.

He leaned in and kissed her deeply, then began to slide them to lay on the floor. He pushed and steered so that he ended up on top of her, pulling the coat over them both until they were tented under the heavy fur, warm and cozy. Drawn by the curve of her chest, he burrowed his way down under the coat until her warm scent filled him. He happily nibbled one lush breast and then the other, feeling her back arch as he gave her pleasure. Then he traveled down her soft belly, licking and kissing lower and lower.

He hadn't done this in Belgium, hadn't needed to. He'd gotten what he wanted with much less effort. Oddly, though, he didn't want to stop this time. He wanted to just keep pleasuring her insanely glorious body as much as he possibly could. He wanted to hear her cry out for him, then he needed to fill her until they both exploded once again. And he realized he wanted to do this over and over, like a teenage boy having sex for the first time, not a world-weary man who had already seduced any number of women.

Her hands wove through his hair, and she lifted herself to him as he tantalized her with his tongue. The muscles in her legs were strong, and he admired her agility. It was easy to guess that nobody had ever done this to her. She half sat, thighs gripping his head, then fell back. Her hands loosened the grip on his hair, and she threw off the fur, stretching her arms and grasping the blanket they lay on.

The cold air hit them, intensifying the erotic feelings, and he crawled back up her body until his gaze met hers. Her legs wrapped around his back as he slipped into her wet warmth. He rose to his knees, pulling her up, chest to breast. He pushed while she pulsed, lifting and lowering. His thighs worked up and down to increase his thrusts, and her muscles tightened in reaction. He didn't think he could keep this up for very long, but he didn't want to stop. The sensations were inconceivably good, and as much as he wished to prolong the pleasure, he knew he couldn't last. Between the stamina it took to continue this amazing position and the control it took to restrain himself, he finally had to let go. She exploded seconds before him and thrashed wildly as she received him, making it all the more pleasurable.

When he was totally spent, he fell to the side, taking her with him. Luckily, they fell onto the coat, making the landing soft and silly, and they each let out an exhausted chuckle. He reached over and gently brushed an errant lock of hair away from her face, letting his fingers linger against the soft skin of her cheek for a moment.

"How do you feel?" His voice came out unusually tender, even to himself.

"I feel . . . I feel . . . I feel ways I've never . . . I feel like a woman," she finally finished.

He gave a little laugh. "Yes, you definitely felt like a woman to me."

Her eyes shone. "I thought you said it wasn't always this good." She chuckled, "Or is that because you knew it was going to feel even better?"

He laughed. "No, really, Miri. It doesn't always feel this good." He rolled toward her and slung an arm across her belly. "Isn't this more fun than games?"

"Yes, more fun than games." She looked at him. "But you are still going to have to play games today. We're not going out in that storm again."

"I think I'd rather go out in the storm." He made a face.

She pushed him, and they began a half-hearted wrestle.

Chapter Twelve: I Want You to Trust Me

"I could beat you. I almost did."

David smiled as Miri laughed at him. "Where did you learn to fight, anyway? I thought you were a peaceful people." He was teasing, yet curious about her skills.

"In games. We have competitions. They're fun."

"Well, you're very good at it. I think I'm bruised." He rubbed his thigh."

"I can kiss it." —she snuggled closer to him—"I can kiss you everywhere . . . at least once, just to make sure."

"Make sure?"

"That I've touched every bit of you with my lips." She sighed. "Every little centimeter."

He felt his body stir. "Miri, you're going to kill me with this." His voice sounded husky, even to his own ears.

"What?" She turned to look up at him, eyes wide.

"It's an expression." His eyes softened. "It means you're going to wear me out with all your loving."

"I want to love you. I feel this thing in my heart, like I want to give all of my being to you." She put her hand to her chest. "It's so strange. Like I would do anything for you."

He peered down at her. "Then, Miri, tell me what you are doing here. Everything you're doing."

"David, I've told you everything I'm doing." Miri raised herself up on one arm. "I've told you more than I should have and shared about things in the future you probably shouldn't

56

know. I may have even twisted time, and I'm scared about it. I'm just praying that you'll never tell another soul any of this." She lay back down and looked up at him. "But I trust you. Time should remain untwisted."

"Is there anything about your research that doesn't have to do with water? Anything to do with governments or weapons?"

"Of course not . . . Well, it has to do with the government. The government is in charge of it all."

"Did they ask you to bring back anything except water?"

"No, just the samples, and I don't even have all of that as it is." She sat up again. "Why are you asking these questions?"

"It just seems strange to me that you would come all this way for only water."

"You think I'm going to hurt you?" She pulled away from him slightly, and her eyes had a shine that spoke of imminent tears.

"No . . . no . . . not you." He put his hand to her face. "I'm just wondering if there's an agenda you might not know about, and they sent you to do their work."

Miri pulled the blanket up in front of her. "I don't understand you. I don't understand how you could think that." She looked away for a moment, then she tapped a finger against her lips. "David, I'll let you look through my things, but you cannot touch the samples, okay?"

He nodded.

"I still don't understand why this is so important to you, but I want you to trust me, because I certainly trust you. Having your trust is more important than almost anything to me except for the water. I must have the water intact. My people must be able to check for plastics." She frowned and looked deep into his eyes. "Will seeing all of my equipment make you feel better?"

"Yes." David swallowed. He felt like someone was kicking

him in the chest. Yep, he got what he wanted. The goal was to have her take him into her confidence, and he had done that. He got the keys to the kingdom, so to speak. He should feel proud of himself. He pushed off the blanket and got to his feet. He quickly got his clothes on and headed for her room. She simply wrapped the blanket around herself and followed him.

"Here." She knelt and put her fingers onto the kit. It snapped open, revealing neat rows of water cups, the dip-sticks he had seen her use, what was left of the perpetuline spindles, and the device used to cut the line. He also identified a small item as another mini-taze and found a few other things he hadn't seen before.

"What's this?" he asked, holding up a cube-shaped item.

"That's what I will use as I go back through the portal. I guess you could call it sort of a key."

David placed it back in the box. "And this?" He held up some packets and shook them. It sounded like powder.

Miri reached out and took one. She ripped it open and poured some of the contents into her mouth. Smacking her lips, she said, "This is what I would have been eating if you hadn't given me food from the cans. Would you like some?" She poured powder onto her palm and offered it up to David.

He paused for a moment, then leaned down and licked the powdery substance from her palm.

Miri giggled. "That feels kind of good."

David smiled. "It doesn't taste so good. Couldn't you do better than that in the future?"

"It's got all the necessary vitamins, electrolytes, and proteins." She raised an eyebrow. "But you're right, it's not very tasty."

"And this?" He lifted a metallic stick.

"Melts down the snow and purifies the water. Makes it safe to drink." She scooted closer. "You see, David, I was all set to

58

get my samples and be fine out here alone, but then you came along. I should have just sent you on your way, but I didn't."

"No, you didn't."

She put one hand on either side of his face and turned him toward her. "I'm glad I didn't. This has been the most wonderful experience of my life. You are complex and confusing and so physically beautiful, and you have made me feel things that I may never feel again."

He gazed back at her, and sadness descended into his very depths. He could feel his face sag.

"What's wrong?"

He shook his head. "Put your kit away."

"You trust me now?" She looked at him with hopeful innocence.

He nodded, then watched her close the kit and slide it against the wall. She was still unclothed, and her vulnerable guilelessness gave him a dull ache. She turned with a glowing smile.

He forced his lips to curve. "How about one of those games?" he asked.

"What's wrong?" She apparently read his face too well.

He cleared his throat. "I . . . I just feel bad for mistrusting you."

"Oh . . . Oh, no." She came over and hugged him to her. "No. I would rather you tell me. We speak our joys, our sorrows, our anger, and our forgiveness. We speak other things, too." She stroked his hair. "You are beloved," she whispered. "So rash and defiant. So sure of yourself, like a child, yet a complex, brilliant man. You make my mind travel to so many places."

She was weaving that magic again, that feeling that no one else had ever given him, as if she could pull all his troubles away. He nestled against her for a moment. Her voice poured over him, soothing, calming, loving.

"Miri," he whispered and encircled her in his arms. They sat that way for a while as she continued to murmur wonderful things to him.

CHAPTER THIRTEEN: LOVE

Later, David conceded to play some of her games. They stacked dried beans on a spoon to see who could hold the most, then raced with those spoons from wall to wall, snickering at the scattered mess. They worked together to build a tower out of plastic cups, then attacked said tower with balled-up paper cannonballs. David found himself laughing uninhibitedly and bounding around like a crazy man.

Instead of spending the day as he ordinarily might have — sealed inside, away from the storm, guzzling whiskey, and staring at the fire — he was chortling with laughter and behaving like a kid. His dignity blew out the window, and he wondered if she still thought he moved like a cat. Certainly, some of the moves he made were more like that of a clumsy boar.

As the afternoon faded toward evening, he dropped onto the couch. "It's a good thing this storm is dying down. I don't think I could stand another day of your crazy games. Give me peace." He raised a palm.

"Never!" she cried and straddled his lap. She put her hands on his shoulders and forced his back against the couch. "You are my prisoner." Her voice was falsely deep and threatening as she brusquely pushed her lips over his and claimed a kiss. He raised his hands to her waist and began to warm to the embrace.

No, don't do it. David had gotten all the information he could get. Miri had let him see her equipment. There was no reason to pull any more Belgium stuff, no more interrogation needed. Still, he continued the kiss.

Her hips began to move, and her thighs pushed against his. His body automatically rose to meet hers. He would stop in a minute. *Just one more minute, and then I'll put an end to this . . .* But he knew he wouldn't, knew he was lost. His breath hitched as the kisses grew more intense.

"I can't get enough," she whispered, sliding off of him and pulling at his shirt. "I want more of you." Her eyes were wild.

David caught her fire. He stood, and suddenly they were tearing at each other's clothes. He paused once they were naked to enjoy the anticipation of touching the flesh in front of him.

Miri dropped to her knees and looked up at him, feeling and probing with her hands. "Men are amazing," she murmured.

Then she licked and stroked and did things that made his knees sway. He buried his hands in her hair and closed his eyes. The throbbing in his body was almost unbearable, but he wanted to make sure her pleasure would match his. He moved down to her level and guided her onto her back, then spent as much time exploring her as she had spent exploring him.

"Women are amazing, too." He smiled and touched her, watching her body react.

He had never done this before, had never really paid attention, but now, he took in everything. He watched the gleam of the fire on her thighs and the soft tones of the flesh on her most private parts. He felt the taut skin of her belly and noted the curves as he moved to her breasts. He took in every bit of her and reveled in the way she touched him. She gazed into his face in a way that made him feel like a wonder of the world. She stroked and kissed and murmured.

As he joined his body with hers, he met her gaze and realized this wasn't sex. This was lovemaking. That was why it felt so different. With that thought, a shudder of intense long-ing and affection ran through him. A desire to consume her, make her his, become one with her, raced through him and settled in his chest even as it roared into his brain. And as it did, he heard her moan through the haze.

"I love you, David. I love you." She rose and gasped as her entire body drew him in.

He gave way to her and answered, "I love you too, Miri." He didn't care. For one abandoned moment, he just didn't care. He did love her. He had to have her.

When they finished, they clung to each other in silence. Did she mean what she said? He didn't know, but it somehow felt right.

Did *he* mean it? How could he? He put his hand to his fore-head. She reached up and stroked his hair.

"I'm all sweaty," he whispered.

"It makes your hair curl." Her eyes sparkled as she looked up at him. "I love you, David. I do."

He smiled down at her. "You're too good for me, Miri."

"That's silly. There is no *too good*. We're all just people. But David . . ."

"Yes?" He caught the seriousness in her voice.

"I have to leave tomorrow, by the end of the day."

"Tomorrow?" He sat up, frowning.

She sat up, too, and nodded. "I have to go tomorrow. If I don't, I'll begin twisting time."

"How do you leave?"

"I go to the portal—it's about a mile away—enter and use my key." Her lips turned down as she moved closer to him, her breast brushing his arm. "If I could stay, I would. If it was just me, I would give up my life to stay with you. But it's not just me." She frowned.

David nodded. He reached out and pulled her to his chest. They sat there silently while he stroked her hair. Every part of his heart hurt.

She slept soundly and innocently as he crept to his room and dragged out the radio.

"Morse! I was wondering if I was going to hear from you. I was afraid the girl did you in. You okay?" Jensen's voice boomed loudly.

David cringed, wondering if Miri had awakened. "Jensen, can you keep your voice down?" He adjusted the volume.

"Sure, sure. Sorry. So, any information from the girl?"

"She knows nothing. She's due to return tomorrow. I don't think there's anything more she can give us."

"Well, we'll see about that. You said she's due to go back tomorrow?"

"Yes."

"Well, good luck for us. The storm's ending, and we'll be at your front door mid-morning. Great job, Morse!"

"I told you, Jensen, there's nothing more to get from her."

"Morse, if she's really from 2165, there's a wealth of technical knowledge she can share. Her equipment alone can be studied by our scientists. And we're sending a doctor to examine her. Body structures must have changed in the coming century. How can you possibly say there's nothing more?"

David knew there was no arguing with Jensen, not when he had that tone of voice, but he was determined to try anyway. "She's not going to tell us anything else. She's been given strict instructions."

"We have our ways, Morse. You know that. She'll share whatever we want her to share. We'll make sure of it. For God's sake, Morse, what's wrong with you?"

David stayed silent.

"You've done a great job. After we pick her up tomorrow, you'll be debriefed, then on your way. I've even arranged for an air force jet to fly you home. Well, as close to home as possible. Then you can pack your bags and be off to the beach. I think you need it. You seem edgy, pal."

"Yeah, out."

"Out."

David packed away the radio then stole back into the living room. Miri still lay sleeping. One leg was thrust out from under the blanket, and one breast showed. *So, they want to examine her, interrogate her, what does it matter to me?* He knew all along that it would come to this, so why couldn't he swallow now?

He needed water. No, he needed whiskey. Whiskey and a cigarette. If she didn't like the smoke, so what? He was finished with her now. Let her cough. He stretched his hands out then flexed his fingers, moving them unconsciously as if tapping an invisible table.

CHAPTER FOURTEEN: IT'S JUST A JOB

Wednesday

David greeted Miri with a tight smile when she awoke. He told her to get dressed and get her things together. Her pained expression let him know that his attitude was tough, but he supposed she believed it was because he was preparing for her to leave.

"I don't have to go until tonight, David. I was hoping . . ."

"Don't hope." He purposely made his voice chilly and his eyes cold. He knew the message he was putting across.

"I don't understand."

"Here, have some breakfast." He shoved a plate at her.

She ate silently, looking up at him now and then. She finally dropped her fork and said, "Can you talk to me about this?"

"Nothing to talk about."

"David," she reached out to touch him, but he pulled away and walked over to the window. She spun in her seat. "David, what's going on?"

Motors roared outside the cabin, and Miri got up off her stool. In moments, the door burst open, and four men in riot gear entered the room raising guns. Miri's eyes widened.

"Come with us, ma'am."

She looked over at David helplessly. "David?" She reached out to him.

The men moved forward, and two of them took her by the arms. The other two patted her down.

"No weapons," one of them announced. "Clear."

"Okay, get her in the APC." They began to pull her.

"David!" she cried out.

Jensen came through the door, walked over to David, then shook his hand. "Great job, Morse."

"An APC, Jensen? Don't you think an armored personnel carrier is a little much for the job?"

Jensen glanced over at Miri and raised his eyebrows. "Maybe. She doesn't look too dangerous." Turning back to David, Jensen smiled and said, "I trust all the coziness didn't wear you out." He slapped David's back, then continued. "The Belgium Method never fails. We'll debrief you, and then you can be on your way."

Miri's eyes grew wider, and her jaw dropped slightly. "David?" she said one more time, this time softly in question.

David looked at her, still keeping his eyes cold, and said, "It's a job, my dear."

His heart almost won over his brain when Miri's knees gave way and two soldiers half-dragged, half-carried her out of the cabin. A third toted her equipment, while a fourth gathered her things from the shed.

"Someone will need to return the snowmobile." David managed to sound professional.

The officer nodded and waved down a soldier.

David rode to Barrow with Jensen in his oversized vehicle. "What now?"

"Oh, now? We'll begin our interrogation. And you'll need to give us a report." Jensen turned to him. "It must have been fascinating—if it is true."

David nodded.

"Do you believe it?"

"I think it's likely."

"Amazing." Jensen shook his head. "I'm anxious to hear

the details. Top secret, of course. Even those boys out there don't know what this is about, no idea who she is." He remained silent for a moment before speaking again. "So, Morse, you'll be going on vacation after this. How long has it been?"

"Four years."

"Yeah, been three for me. That's how it is for men like us." Jensen's tone turned jovial. "You're one of the best, Morse. Everyone says that."

"Do they?"

"Oh yes. They've made a legend of you," Jensen chuckled. "You'd better be careful."

"I'm hardly legend material." David turned and looked out the window. "So where is it that we're going?"

"Underground bunker in Barrow. Tight security — unknown to either friends or enemies. Best place until we can get her on a plane to London."

"And when will that be?"

"Couple of days. There's a whole list of people who want to see her. Talk to her. Examine her. Get information from her. And, of course, we'll have to share her with DC when we get finished with her. Who knows where else she'll go."

David looked down, staring at his fur gloves, clenched into tight fists.

Chapter Fifteen: Unbearable

Thursday

David awoke with a headache. Or was it something else? There was another pain. Something he didn't want to think about.

He wanted a drink. First thing in the morning, a drink. He pulled his clothes on and didn't bother combing his hair, then stumbled down to the hotel bar and found it open. *Happy days!* He winced at the phrase that popped into his head.

He sat at the bar and ordered, "Give me a double scotch."

The bartender was the quiet type, fortunately, and served him without comment. David knocked it back, then asked for another. A waitress peeked in and asked if he'd like some breakfast.

"No, not really," he answered, but then ordered some toast.

He continued drinking throughout the morning, then stumbled back upstairs to his room. He was glad he was headed for a vacation. His inebriated state was a sure sign he needed it. He had never started off his day drunk before . . . ever. That was his last thought before he conked out.

Someone shook David's shoulder, and he leaped out of bed, grabbed the gun from under his pillow, then pinned the intruder against the dresser, pistol to their forehead.

The wide-eyed soldier raised his hands. "Ensign Porter, sir. Please don't shoot. I'm sorry, but you didn't answer the phone or the door, so they asked me to have the manager un-lock it for a room check."

David leaned back and pulled the gun away. "I apologize. I was just surprised. I guess I was sleeping too heavily."

"Yes, sir." The soldier nodded genially. "They asked me to let you know that you are needed for debriefing at 1400 hours, sir."

"Please tell them I am not well and that I'll be available for debriefing tomorrow."

"Not well, sir?"

"Not well." He gave the soldier a cold stare, realizing that with his unshaven face and wild hair, he probably looked like he was out of his mind. That was fine with him. Between how frightening he must look and the man nearly getting shot, the soldier would likely not push him.

"As you say, sir. I'll let them know you will not be available until tomorrow, sir." He saluted and left, quietly closing the door behind him.

David lay back down on the bed. He turned on his side. Everything still hurt, only it wasn't physical. "Ohhh . . ." He groaned and grabbed a pillow. Pressing it into his belly, he curled up around it. He had been tortured in his time, badly enough to leave scars. He'd had his hand thrust into fire, his solar plexus pummeled like a punching bag. He'd had his head bashed countless times, but nothing came close to what he endured now. It was almost unbearable.

Friday

David had expected anger, cynicism, bitterness, or maybe tears, but when he was let into the room with Miri, she looked up at him and her face softened almost into a smile.

"David." Her eyes radiated tenderness.

"You're coming with me." He reached out and grabbed her arm, roughly pulling her to her feet without resistance. He banged on the door, and it opened. "I'm taking her for a walk." The guard looked doubtful but let them pass.

David dragged Miri down the hall then turned the corner. Her things sat on the floor where David had left them after retrieving them from the next room.

Without a word, Miri tore off her hospital garb and slid on her sweater, leggings, and outerwear. David was already dressed for the trip, wearing his fur jacket and boots.

He strode quickly and purposefully, dragging Miri at a half-run behind him as he hurried out to the heliport. He opened flaps in the first and second helicopters, yanking cords from each as he went and tossing them to the ground. Finally, he helped her into the third helicopter. He climbed in and showed her how to fasten the safety harness and put on the goggles and headphones.

The machine roared to life and, within minutes, they lifted into the air. He flew the copter toward Snow Owl Cabin, asking her exactly where they needed to go. She gave him the coordinates. Wind coming from the open doorway blew her hair in gales of wild beauty, and she smiled as she looked at the view below.

His belly began to loosen, and he reached out, grasping her leg. He was warmed by a glow in her eyes, one he could see even through the goggles, and he smiled down at her.

Before long, he reached the portal area and set the bird down gently, then helped her out. She pulled her key from the kit, then re-shouldered the strap.

Miri stepped in the direction of the portal, then suddenly stopped and pulled off the goggles. "David?"

He tore his goggles off and looked back at her. "Miri."

"David, I love you."

"How? How could you?"

"It's easy."

He reached out and grabbed her, holding her so tightly he

was afraid she wouldn't be able to breathe.

"David? Do you have a picture? I know I shouldn't . . . but do you have a picture I can take back with me?"

He dug in his pocket. In his wallet was one photo of him with his mother. He hated to part with it. In order to keep his mother from danger after he had started his job with the bureau, he had rarely visited her. Now, this was the only photo he had left of the two of them together.

"Here. This is me with my mother. It was taken about five years ago, right before she passed." He pressed it into Miri's hand.

Miri reached up to stroke his hair and kissed him, then she moved toward a clear space and twisted the cube. He watched her flicker and fade even as she kept her gaze on his.

Saturday

"Morse." Jensen's voice crackled over the Snow Owl radio.

David walked into the bedroom to answer. His footsteps seemed to echo in the lonely cabin. "Good morning, Jensen."

"You know, Morse, you've set yourself up for international action. Court-martial type action."

"Possibly." David countered.

"Possibly." Jensen's heavy sigh came through the radio loud and clear.

"You'd have to supply a full report as to why."

"Yes."

"With proof."

"Yes."

"You've got proof, of course . . . of visitors from the future?" David couldn't help the lilt in his voice.

"Bring that helicopter in, then go have a nice vacation, Morse."

David could imagine Jensen shaking his head. "Thanks, Jensen." He smiled. "Out."

"Out."

PART II—DECEMBER 1959

CHAPTER SIXTEEN: LIFE HANGS IN THE BALANCE

Peter Smith, a young British operative—who also carried passports under the names David Morse, David Stone, David Porter, Patrick Drake, Joseph Serf, and several other monikers—made his way through the cold fog that shrouded Stornoway. He had taken a ferry to this little Scottish island town several days prior. The inn where he was staying was rustic but pleasant, and he was now headed to Old McNeill's to have a light meal and a round or two of authentic Scotch whiskey.

Admiral Jensen had briefed him on the odd circumstances in the area. A senior aircraftman at the early warning RAF radar station, Aird Uig, had seen what he described as a *tiny dot in the sky that grew larger and larger*. It had flown past camp with a roar, trailing smoke, and sped over the horizon. It had been headed for an area near Stornoway where two lochs were located.

Of course, they'd sent out an exploration party to determine what the thing was. A comet? Some sort of new enemy weapon? What they'd found was a dry patch of land where one of the lochs had previously been. All the water appeared to have been drained out of that loch, and the area looked as if there had been an earthquake. A searing smell had lingered in the air.

Jensen had sent Hugh Butler, a well-known astrophysicist, out to Stornoway to examine the area. Unfortunately, Hugh had found no fragments or evidence of an impact, so he couldn't confirm anything. This had concerned Jensen, so he called on Peter to travel to Stornoway to investigate.

"This could be some sort of new weapon," Jensen had said. "Go, check it out, and give me a full report."

With plenty of media interest flocking around the area, it had been easy for Peter to slip in undercover as a journalist. In his guise as a reporter, he had been poking around, and everybody seemed eager to help him. With all the stories and photos going out, they hoped they'd be mentioned when he went to publish his piece.

Peter pulled his collar up around his neck and shoved his hands into his pockets. The weather had been extreme in November, and it looked as if December was going to be tough as well.

Peter's footsteps echoed in the bitter air as he walked through the Narrows, but then he heard another set of steps behind him. The other footfalls sped up. Peter slowed in response and girded himself . . . just in case. Everything was always *just in case* in this business. Too frequently, it turned out to be somebody approaching him, ready to do him harm.

When the footsteps closed the distance, Peter turned, prepared to deflect a blow or kick out at a wielded gun—whatever might be required. He was surprised when a woman emerged from the soupy fog, then stopped and stared up at him.

"Good evening." He greeted her with a smile and tipped his hat.

"David?" Her gaze fixed on his.

He noted the question in her expression, her frown, and the weariness in her gaze. A sadness seemed to float around her even as her long dark hair gently lifted in the bitter breeze. The bangs on her forehead ruffled with the wind, and he wondered how she could be warm enough in the light coat she was wearing.

"I'm afraid my name is Peter—Peter Smith." He reached out a hand to shake, but she ignored it.

"I have some important information for you." Her voice sounded tense, and she continued to look him straight in the eyes.

"Do you?" He kept his voice light and gave a slight smile.

"It's urgent," she said, unrelenting.

"Let's go someplace we can talk," he suggested. "I was on my way to the pub. Would you care to join me?" He put one hand lightly under her elbow and gestured with the other.

She gave a doubtful look, then finally nodded.

As they continued through the Narrows toward McNeill's, Peter tried to make light conversation. "I haven't seen you in Stornoway before. Have you been here long?"

She shook her head.

"Where are you from?"

"It doesn't matter, David . . . Peter."

He glanced down at her. "Who is David?" Had he met her somewhere when he had been using one of his other identities? Narrowing his eyes, he went through his memory, but no, he was sure he had never met this woman before. He'd remember a woman like her—well built, unique features, unusual hair. He guessed she was about his age, possibly older, about thirty. No, he wouldn't have forgotten this one.

"David is somebody I knew once," she murmured.

"And here we are." Peter opened the pub door and ushered her inside. The interior glow brought a sudden warmth that broke some of the tension between them, and Peter led her to a private booth near the back. He slipped off his coat and took hers, still amazed that she could wear such a light thing in this weather, then hung them on the hook. "What can I get you?"

"Oh . . . Uh, whiskey." Her pronunciation was odd, as if

she wasn't quite familiar with the word.

"Scotch whiskey?" he asked. "It's quite fine here."

"Okay." She looked bewildered.

He came back to the table with two glasses and slid into his side of the booth.

"Do you have a name?" He smiled.

"Miri."

"Just Miri? No last name?"

"It's Smith. Just like you."

"I see." He gave a tight grin and raised his glass. "Well, here's to you, Miri Smith."

She picked up her glass, also raised it, and took a small sip. Her cough and grimace told him that she was not an experienced drinker.

"Water?"

She nodded. He got up and grabbed a couple glasses of water for them.

"Thank you." She took a few gulps.

"You're not a whiskey drinker?"

"It's been a while." Then she finally gave him a tiny smile. "I liked it when I was here, though."

"Oh, you've been to Stornoway before?"

She shook her head, "Not *here*—just here." And she took another sip. "Whiskey makes one feel so good. I remember that." A dreamy look came over her eyes. "But . . ." She glanced back at him, all business again. "I have to talk to you."

"Okay." He nodded genially. "What can I do for you?"

"You have to listen to me, and you have to listen carefully." She leaned forward. "Life hangs in the balance."

CHAPTER SEVENTEEN: WHO ARE YOU?

Peter straightened in his seat. Perhaps she had inside information about this so-called comet. Maybe it was something much more than a comet.

"You have to believe what I am going to tell you." She leaned forward, her gaze intense.

"Okay." He cocked his head to the side and gave a half-smile, trying to break the tension.

"You are going to meet me again in the future."

Smith frowned. "When? Why?"

She shook her head. "It doesn't matter. Just know that you are."

He tried to determine the status of her sanity.

"And when you do," she continued, "you must get me to my destination on the day I am supposed to be there. Do you understand?"

"Get you to your destination? What destination?"

"You'll know when it happens."

"I don't understand."

"Don't betray me this time. You *cannot* betray me." She frowned, and her fingernails gently dug into the tabletop. "It's not for my sake, David. I could have sustained anything for you, but you *must not* betray me this time."

"Why would I betray you?" He shook his head. "I don't know what you're talking about. My name's not David. I think you have me confused—"

She cut him off. "We both know that you're David Morse,

at least sometimes. We both know about your . . . your . . . *Belgium Method*."

He went pale. "I have no idea —"

"And when you meet me again, you will remember this conversation, and you will remember other things, foggy things — at least a little bit — but I . . . I will not. I will not remember you at all, so you will have to make sure." She was speaking so quickly it was almost a ramble. "You'll have to make sure that I get there on the tenth day. Do you understand?"

"No."

She drank a bigger gulp of her whiskey, then looked back up at him. He continued staring at her. *How does she know such things about me?* She could possibly know his David Morse identity from some encounter or from some other agent. But the Belgium Method? That was a joke, a terrible cynical joke, that Jensen had made up. A label he had put on a strategy Peter had used in Belgium to get information desperately needed from a woman when he'd had no other choice.

Then he'd had to do the same thing again in Lithuania. Still, Jensen continued to call it the *Belgium Method*, making Peter a little sick to his stomach until it finally just became part of the job. But nobody else knew about it, and if anyone overheard him say it, they would have no idea of its meaning. Had someone been able to tap into their encoded transmissions?

Peter threw back a slug of whiskey and drummed his fingers on the table. "Are you staying at the inn?"

She shook her head.

"Where are you staying?"

"Around."

"Look, come back with me, and we'll talk in a more private atmosphere. I need to ask you some questions."

"I can't trust you — who you are now. I'm just hoping I can trust you later." She continued nursing her whiskey.

"How do I know I can trust *you*?" he asked her. "You have a lot of information, and I don't even know how you got it."

She looked up at him with a slight grin. "*You* gave it to me . . . And what you didn't tell me, I got from . . . from someone named Jennings or Jensing or something like that."

"Jensen?"

"That might have been it. It's been over five years."

"Five years? I've only been working with Jensen for three."

"Look, David . . . Peter, I don't expect you to understand any of this right now, but you will. And when you do, I just ask that you make sure I get to my destination at the right time. I *cannot* be late."

He peered down at her and leaned back, frowning and stroking his chin as he considered what she was telling him. It all seemed so far-fetched, yet she appeared sincere, almost desperate.

Silence reigned between them as they continued to scrutinize each other. Miri's gaze traveled across his face, and her expression softened. She reached across the table and gently drew the tip of her finger down the side of his cheek. He resisted the impulse to pull away. He didn't know her. He wasn't sure he wanted to be touched by this stranger. He almost felt intimidated by her, but he forced himself to do what was necessary to make her believe he accepted what she said.

"Your face remains breathtaking. It's just slightly different, smoother, less weathered. Your eyes are still like from the gods, and your lips . . ." She stopped, and her gaze came back into focus as she clearly pulled herself together.

"Come back to the inn with me," he said gently. "We'll talk this out. You can explain it better."

"Sure." She nodded.

He helped her on with her coat, and they exited the pub into the gloomy night. He guided her with his hand on her arm, half to keep her safe from falling and half to make sure she couldn't run. The walk was quiet, and he stole a few glances down at her serious brow, catching her features behind the mist forming in the air.

There was something odd about the woman. Her accent wasn't American and wasn't British, but he couldn't quite place it. She certainly felt an urgency about whatever she was trying to convey. He would doubt her sanity except for the fact she had knowledge of things no one should know. Once they got to his room, he would have to dig deeper. He had a bottle stashed up there. If she was an inexperienced drinker, a few more shots of whiskey might loosen her tongue.

Before long, they were inside his cozy little room. He perched on the edge of the bed while Miri sat back on an easy chair by the wall. He poured her a generous shot of whiskey and did the same for himself.

He leaned forward, resting his elbows on his knees, the glass between his hands. "Now, can you explain this to me again?"

She shook her head. "No. I can't tell you any more than what I've already said. If you understood everything, you might be more willing to believe. On the other hand, I can't trust you. If I explain it all, it's quite possible you could destroy a life while convincing yourself you're doing the right thing." She bit her lip. "Just remember to get me to the destination and don't betray me. That's all you need to know. Telling you this much is risky. Even attempting this whole thing is risky, but there seemed to be no other way."

"Risky? How? What is the risk?"

Leaning back and resting her head against the chair, she took a long gulp of her whiskey and said, "Please, David . . . Peter, there's no more to say. Your world is full of people." She closed her eyes. "My world doesn't have so many people. Each life is valuable, because we don't have so many people like you do. Before my time, there were pandemics, catastrophes, famines, but the life hanging in the balance right now is particularly precious. In order to preserve that, I need to get back at just the right moment."

"I don't understand what you're talking about. None of it makes any sense. But what's most important to me right now is how you have knowledge of certain specifics from classified conversations I've had with my superior."

Miri opened her eyes and looked over at him. "It'll all make sense in the end. You just need to remember *this* conversation when the time comes."

He set his drink down on the nightstand, then went over to her. With one hand on each arm of her chair, he hovered over her, pressing down and scowling to intimidate her. "You *will* talk to me, Miss Smith, either voluntarily or not-so-voluntarily, but I need some questions answered." He peered into her eyes. "Will this be easy, or will you make it difficult?"

Miri looked up at him, and before he could take a breath, she lifted her thigh, raised a foot, and kicked, making him double over. She was on her feet in a flash and knocked him to the ground. He heard a clicking noise and felt a course of electricity go through him that left him unable to move. He lay there, not even able to groan.

She leaned over him and said, "I don't have the energy for this." She pulled him by the shoulders until his head was resting in her lap. "Please believe me, David. I just don't have it in me anymore. You don't know what I've been through." Then she ran her fingers through his hair, pushing it off his forehead.

"What *was* that?" he managed to whisper.

"A mini-taze." She sighed and looked down into his face. "I wish . . . I wish . . ." She leaned forward and kissed his cheek.

He looked back up at her. *What does she wish?*

"Look . . ." she said and reached into a pocket. "I'm going to give you this because I want you to believe me." She pulled out a piece of paper. "But you have to give it back to me when we meet again, because it's mine." She held it out to him.

He could finally move a little, so he reached up and took it. Raising it up to view, he saw it was a photo of him and his mother. *But how can this be? I haven't seen Mother in two years. No photo like this has ever been taken. And my hair is all wrong. My hairline is slightly receded.*

"This was taken right before your mother died," Miri said.

He frowned up at her. "She's not dead."

Miri nodded. "When you meet me next time, you will remember things that I will not. That's the way it must be in order to change the outcome. It's a risk for you, David, but if you *really* understood, I know it's a risk you would gladly take. You need to make sure that I get there. Don't betray me. It's not for my sake." She pushed him a little as she slid out from under his shoulders.

He struggled to gain a seated position. "Who *are* you?" He tried to shake the dizziness from his head. "Do you have something to do with the comet?"

She flashed a small smile. "I had to get you here somehow. This watery place has a doorway for us." Without another word, she quietly exited his room.

Peter pulled himself onto the bed, not quite sure how to process this meeting. She had used a kind of small weapon on him that he had never before encountered. She had spoken things that were confusing, yet they frighteningly made plenty of sense if you pieced them together with impossible ideas. He couldn't report back to Jensen that the mystery comet appeared because some crazy woman from the . . . the . . . future wanted to draw him to Stornoway. He supposed he'd just have to continue investigating to see if he could come up with a real reason, then report back with that — or nothing.

Nothing was what he came up with, and nothing more seemed to go on in the Stornoway area, so Jensen eventually sent him on to more urgent assignments.

PART III—EARLY NOVEMBER 1967

Chapter Eighteen: A Feeling of Déjà Vu

Thursday

David boarded the plane at Thule Air Force base, annoyed and cold. He had hoped to be headed for vacation on a warm Mediterranean beach someplace, not waylaid on a mission to yet another arctic wasteland. He didn't relish the journey. This flight would last through the night, then a charter plane, then finally a snowmobile ride. At least it wasn't a dogsled. He'd have no real rest until he was at the frigid cabin north of Barrow.

"Are you comfortable, Mr. Morse?"

David nearly flinched when a young Airman leaned down to offer him a blanket. From the moment he'd boarded this plane, something felt off. The Airman somehow seemed familiar. It was as if David knew exactly how the man was going to lean and exactly the words he would use. It was unnerving. David took the blanket and stretched it as best he could over his long frame. It was going to be tough to get some sleep.

Friday

Hours later, David was shaken awake by the same Airman. Mystified, he staggered to the bathroom and tried to figure out why everything seemed to be an echo of something that had happened before.

The rest of his journey went as smoothly as he expected and he reached Snow Owl Cabin as the afternoon sky was beginning to darken. Still, he couldn't shake his discomfort.

The key to the cabin was exactly where his handler, Jensen, had told him it would be, but he would have known its location even if Jensen had said nothing. He also knew he would have to jiggle the lock before it yielded to him.

Once he gained access, he stomped the snow off his boots and beat his mittened hands together. It was only after he got the generator going and had a fire built that he took a good look around. He paced the floor, gulping hot tea laced with a liberal dose of whiskey. The inside of the place looked exactly as he had anticipated, down to minute details. He wanted to chalk it up to the fact that all small cabins probably looked the same inside. *But do all little cabins have a stuffed white owl up by the fireplace? Do they all have a breakfast bar between the kitchen and the dining area? Do they all have exactly one couch and two easy chairs with an Indian print rug in front of the fireplace?* Those precise little details were not something he should know. He had never been in this place before, but somehow, he was completely aware of what would be here before he stepped inside.

He plunked down in an easy chair and let the cold ease out of his bones. Fatigue was setting in even as he still pondered this unusual experience. He supposed, however, that it was time to shelve such thoughts and figure out his sleeping arrangement. It wouldn't do him any good to doze off in the chair.

He forced himself up and headed into the kitchen to wash his cup, but something outside the window caught his eye. *What the hell? Smoke in the distance?* The last thing he wanted to do was go back out into that cold, but something waited for him there. A shudder ran through his body, and his heart raced. *What a ridiculous thought. Yeah, something might very well be waiting, just not in the predestined way floating through my mind.* He had to go find out exactly what was out there. That was his job, wasn't it? He headed for his boots and coat.

There was no disguising the noise of the snowmobile, so he didn't even try. When he caught sight of a dome-shaped tent in the distance, he headed straight for it. *Who would be camping out here in this weather, especially this time of year?* As he got closer, a small figure emerged from the odd structure.

"Hello," he called out.

"Hi," a young woman yelled back and waved.

"What is all this? What are you doing out here?" His words whipped around in the wind, but she seemed to make out what he asked.

Her hands cupped around her mouth as she shouted her answer. "Research."

He climbed off the snowmobile and approached her with a strange sense of having done this before. "Look, I've got a little cabin just over the way. It might be warmer for you."

Some fierce force inside him insisted that if she refused to come with him, he would have to compel her to do so. One thing he felt certain of was that she had to come to the cabin. This need had nothing to do with the mission. This was something more profound. He shook his head, trying to refocus on the conversation.

The girl looked doubtful, then glanced back at her tent and shrugged. "I suppose it can't hurt anything."

Before he could offer to help her, she was packing her gear. With a flick of her hand, she collapsed her tent, then all her things fit nicely into a small cart on skis that could easily be towed behind them.

It didn't take long to get back to the cabin. The woman rode behind him and held on as the snowmobile moved across the small hills. The feel of her arms wrapped around his waist made him shiver, even though his fur jacket was warm. The effect she had on him was unnerving, and when they got to the cabin, he couldn't climb off the snowmobile fast enough.

Once they got inside, he regained his composure. "I don't think I've seen equipment like yours before. Very unique."

"Yes, I guess it is. Thank you."

Her accent seemed vaguely familiar.

"Where is it manufactured?"

"Sana Mundi"

"Sana Mundi?" He searched his memory. "Where is that again? I know I've heard of it."

"It's not well known to people around here." She walked over to the window. "It's really cold out there, isn't it?"

David nodded, not missing the fact that she never gave him a clear answer. "I've got extra blankets if you need them."

She turned around and smiled. "No, my sleeping gear is quite warm, thank you."

They stared at each other silently for so long that David felt an awkwardness creep into the air. At the same time, it was as if he was grasping at thoughts, like when one attempts to find just the right word and can't quite get it. The girl looked up at him, studying his face.

"Well" — he cleared his throat — "why don't you get settled, then we can have a drink."

She nodded, then disappeared into her room. David went into his and straightened his bed, then meandered back toward the kitchen,

"Would you care for a drink?" He called as she emerged from her room.

She was a good-looking woman, and it suddenly struck him that she was the woman he'd met back in Stornoway, that odd one, the one who gave him the photo. Only now, she seemed to be at least five years younger, not eight years older.

"Some water would be nice," she said.

He tried to smile but was studying her. "I was thinking maybe something warmer . . . like whiskey."

"Whiskey?"

"Yes." He raised the bottle and gently waved it, lifting his eyebrows in question. "Whiskey. Would you like some?" *She had drunk whiskey in Stornoway and had known what it was then. How could she not know it now?*

"Okay. I'll have some of that."

"By the way, what's your name?" He poured them each a glass.

"Miri."

"Miri?"

She nodded.

"Just . . . Miri? Don't you have a last name?"

"Um, yes . . . Smith."

"Miri Smith." He stretched out the words and nodded. "Of course." He handed her the drink, then raised his glass, saying, "Well, *Miri Smith* . . . cheers." He had this conversation before. *How many times before?*

"Cheers." She followed his lead, raising her glass, then she brought it to her lips and sipped. "Oh!" She coughed. "This is alcohol." She grimaced. "And it's strong."

"It's whiskey. Come on, you *know* whiskey. I know you know whiskey. *Scotch* whiskey." He bit his lip and frowned. "Whiskey — it'll keep you warm."

"I guess *that's* true." She took another sip, "Happy days!" She shook her head. "It feels good. And it *does* keep one warm."

"Come and sit down." He waved her into the living room. "Tell me, where are you from?" He tried to be casual, charming, relaxed.

"Oh, around."

"Barrow?"

"No, not Barrow. And you?" She gripped her whiskey tightly at first, but as she sipped, she leaned back, and her grasp seemed to loosen.

"I'm not from Barrow either." He raised his drink in a mock

toast and smiled. "And what kind of research are you doing, may I ask?" He fought back the sarcastic tone creeping into his voice.

"Water research. I'm a Socio-ecological Hydrologist."

"What does one do when they are a Socio-ecological Hydrologist." He frowned, feeling as though he could answer his own questions.

"Study water to find out what conditions impact ecology."

"And who are you doing this research for?"

"Our government."

"*Our* government?"

"Yours and mine. The World Government."

"The world?" He felt like a man with a shadow. Like an invisible version of himself had lived this moment just a fraction of a second or maybe a million years before. It was as if he had always known this woman, but at the same time, had only just met her. The sight of her was making his heart race, nearly bringing tears to his eyes, but she looked at him warily, with no recognition.

"Miri . . ." he began.

"Yes."

"Do you remember meeting me previously?"

She frowned and shook her head. "No."

He let the subject go. His meeting with Miri in Stornoway had come back to him completely, and he had a tight feeling in his belly. Something very different was happening here. If he believed in déjà vu, which he didn't, he'd almost think he was experiencing it.

Once they each retired for the night, he got on the short wave to Jensen. "Do you have any knowledge of Socio-hydrology studies going on up here?

"Socio-hydrology? What in the world, Morse?"

"No, take that back, Socio-*ecological* Hydrology."

"No, I know nothing about studies up there, and I've never even heard of that."

"Well, I found this woman, all alone. She claims to be a researcher in Socio-ecological Hydrology. She has some very unique equipment."

"Who does she work for?"

"The *World Government*, whatever that means. And she says she's from Sana Mundi. It sounds familiar, but I couldn't place it on a map. See what you can find out."

"Will do."

"Thanks. I'll check back with you tomorrow with any updates."

Later that night, David stood outside her door, listening to the sound of her long breaths. Certain she was sleeping soundly, he crept in to get a look at her gear. Somehow, he already knew he wouldn't be able to get into it. He had a feeling in his gut that he had tried this before, and he *remembered* the kit was sealed with no apparent opening. He would have to wait until morning and see if he could assist with her so-called research.

Equipment forgotten, David stood and watched Miri sleep. Darts of pleasure drove through his body until it became difficult not to reach over and touch her. He *knew* this woman, and not just from Stornoway. He knew her much more intimately than that.

Like a lost childhood recollection, moments with her were emerging from some sort of fog, yet he had no physical memories of her that he was aware of. Still, he knew her body, her kiss, her touch. And recalling those things, his own body reacted so intensely he had to force himself to turn away. He went to his room, finally ending up in a steamy shower to do away with the pent-up hormones that would otherwise certainly disturb his sleep.

Chapter Nineteen: You Got Lucky

Saturday

David heard Miri moving about the kitchen. After dressing, he padded out and saw her staring at the cans in her hands, seemingly baffled. *Of course, she wouldn't know what to do with them.*

"There's a can opener in the left-hand drawer." He chuckled, then sleepily trod over, pulled out the can opener, and showed her how to work it.

He had to demonstrate several things in the kitchen and was unsurprised to hear that the strange place she came from didn't use cans or plastics. He was beginning to get used to his sudden embedded knowledge. Her unusual, almost deranged ideas were ones he had heard before . . . from her. He just couldn't figure out *when* he had heard them . . . or *how.*

He suspected he had possibly been the victim of some sort of enemy mind manipulation. Maybe drugged and hypnotized, told under hypnotic trance that all of this was going to happen, and now it was playing out. She could be a very good actress. She spoke with odd phrases, as if English was not her first language. Who could she be working for? Had they sent this woman to scope out a vulnerable spot for a nuclear missile base? Which government would do that? It could be any. This location would be a perfect place to put both the United States and Russia in danger. Where was Sana Mundi anyway?

Why, however, would they have picked him for this strategic mind manipulation? Back in 1959, when she had given him that photograph, he had been talented and successful but just beginning to make his mark.

How did she get that picture of him with his mother before the fact? And how did she know the things she did about him? Even more peculiar, she appeared to not know him now, and she looked several years younger. Was she not the same girl? A sister perhaps?

Had he been hypnotized to believe that the meeting in 1959 took place? Had he never met her in Stornoway at all? That idea unnerved him, but he quickly realized the Stornoway meeting *must* have happened. He had been walking around with two of those photos in his pocket for five years now. One of them he got from her eight years ago. The other was taken with his mother right before she died. The two photos were identical, but from different times. The only way that could be possible was —

Miri emerged from her room wearing the same outfit she'd worn when he'd found her at her camp.

"Is that going to be enough for you?" he asked, nodding toward her jacket.

"Certainly. This is completely insulated fabric, good for temperatures as low as negative forty-five degrees Celsius. That's about fifty degrees below in Fahrenheit."

"I know," he answered with a smirk. But inside, he realized that he also knew all about that fabric. It was made from something she had once called *Thinsulate*.

He joined her on her research trek, and they trudged west. "We're going to the water?" he stated more than asked.

"Yes. Like I said, I need to collect samples."

"Of water?"

"Yes."

It was difficult to carry on a conversation with their mouths covered, plus he had a difficult time keeping up with her as she strutted along. He admired her grace as she seemed to float over the snow, and he recalled how she had put him down on the floor in Stornoway. She was strong and agile. A quick flash of her body in firelight snapped through his mind. *Wishful thinking, or . . .*

They got to the water's edge, and she unfolded the top of each boot so that her thighs were covered halfway up. Then she stepped forward, opened her kit, and drew out a dipping stick. She scooped up water from the depths and poured samples into individual cups. *Why is this scene so familiar?*

Once she was finished, she packed up, slung the kit over her shoulder, and turned toward him. "Finished." And she headed back to the cabin with him trailing her once again.

"I thought you said you needed help," he called out, trying to keep up with her.

"I guess I didn't." She glanced back at him, smiling.

"You were playing with me."

She laughed. "What else have you got to do? Drink whiskey?"

He grinned, but at the same time, he heard laughter as if coming from some other world. He almost covered his ears to stop it but realized it was his own laughter. He shivered, but not from the cold. Something was impacting his senses.

Once they were inside, Miri looked up at him with a frown, "Are you chilled even now? Maybe you should leave your things on."

David shook his head. "No, I'm fine." He hung his coat on the rack, then pulled off his boots.

Miri reached out and pulled back the edge of his jacket, examining it. "I've read about these. Killing and cutting up beasts for their hides. Strange. It is quite nice to touch, though."

"You haven't ever heard of a fur coat?"

"We don't have them where I come from."

"Where *do* you come from, Miri?" David was tired of

games and was certainly tired of how confused he felt.

"It would be hard for you to understand, David." She turned and headed toward the kitchen. "Let's make lunch."

The rest of the afternoon was spent in casual conversation. The odd feeling of familiarity persisted as David attempted to discover more about Miri's work and her origins.

Later, in his room, he radioed Jensen. "Did you find out anything?"

"Nothing. No universities offering Socio-ecological Hydrology, and no women having received degrees from anything close to that. And no country called Sana Mundi. You struck out on every point, Morse. You're losing your touch. You've got to get more information about what's going on there."

"Well, she's not exactly forthcoming with her agenda."

"No? Well, remember Belgium . . . Lithuania . . . Madagascar?"

David closed his eyes. "Yes, of course."

"Try that."

"Yeah, sure. Whatever it takes. But I hate doing that." He sighed.

"Oh yeah, it's so tough," Jensen's voice mocked him, "I wish I had it so tough. That's like a vacation in itself, buddy. Hell, it's better than a vacation."

David ground his teeth. "Not really, Jensen. But I'll get you the information."

"And, Morse, you got *extra* lucky."

"In what way?"

"There's a huge storm heading toward Snow Owl tomorrow afternoon. You two should be locked in nice and cozy for a couple days. You've got enough supplies, right?"

"Yeah, but it's not what I'd call lavish."

Jensen snorted. "You'll survive. I'm getting together a

team. We'll be on the way up there to take the girl into custody. But we won't move in until you're finished with her."

"Got it."

Chapter Twenty: We've Done This Before

Sunday

David jolted awake to a light tap on his shoulder. Leaping from his bed, he pushed Miri up to the dresser, a pistol crushed against her head.

"Happy days, David! Do you always wake up like that?" Her eyes were wide.

"No ... No." He put the gun down. "I'm sorry." He couldn't meet her eyes.

Miri reached out and gently touched him. "It's okay."

He looked up, and her gaze was frank. *Is she comforting me?* Her hand was still on his arm, and he felt the warmth drift upward.

She smiled, "I made breakfast."

They went into the kitchen, and he looked at the food she had prepared, a remarkably tasty goulash.

After breakfast, she went to her room, emerging a short time later to let him know it was time to collect her samples.

"How do you manage to fit all your equipment into that one kit?" he asked.

"It was specially made."

"How does it open?" He examined it as if this were the first time.

"Only to my fingerprints."

"Really? Why so secretive?"

"Oh, not secretive. It's fast and efficient." She shrugged it off. "Are you going to join me again, or is it too much for you?"

Her eyes sparkled with a mischievous light that made his heart skip a beat. As much as he hated wandering around in the cold, he wanted . . . no, needed . . . to be with her. He felt a compulsion to stay by her side, no matter what.

"I wouldn't miss it for the world."

After they'd collected the samples and returned to the cabin, the afternoon lay ahead of them. David offered Miri another whiskey, and she accepted. She still shuddered with her first few sips, but her laughter let him know that she was beginning to enjoy it.

"Happy days! I'll get addicted to this drink." She stretched and leaned back on the couch. "People don't drink very much where I come from."

"Well, they drink very much here." He chuckled and moved closer to her, suggestively asking, "And how shall we spend our afternoon?"

Instead of falling into his trap, she insisted upon a competition game. He soon found himself on his knees, racing to see who could blow a balled-up piece of paper across the floor the fastest.

Although the game was familiar, he still felt embarrassed and idiotic, but what choice did he have? He needed to loosen her up, make her a friend.

When she beat him, she turned around, face flushed and laughing. "Happy days! You're going to have to move faster than that. Don't you know how to blow?"

He crawled up next to her and leaned against the wall. "No, I haven't blown paper balls across floors in a very long time."

"Well, it was fun." She put her hand to her neck as she met

his gaze.

He reached out. He had been waiting for this moment — knew it was coming — the moment he could finally touch her hair. He paused for half a second, then pushed a stray lock from her face with the back of his hand. "My idea of fun might be something a little more . . . grown up."

She blushed. "I don't know if I'm old enough for grown-up things."

"You're twenty-four, Miri. Right?" There was no doubt in his mind.

She nodded.

"You're a woman, a spectacularly beautiful woman."

Miri trembled. "I'm still young."

"You're old enough to know there's something odd going on here. Please, Miri." David scowled. "You have *got* to tell me what it is. What are you doing here? What are you doing to *me*? I *have* to know."

"To *you*, David? Nothing to you. None of this has anything to do with you." She rose to her feet. "I'll be leaving in a few days anyway."

He followed behind her.

"I need you to open up your gear for me."

She shook her head. "My research is too important. I can't have you tampering with it." Dropping her gaze, she continued, "I'm sorry."

He walked over and grabbed her by the wrist, holding her hand in the air. "So am I. You're going to have to open it for me."

They struggled as he tried to force her over to the box, intending to place her fingertips on it, but she suddenly pulled against him. He knew what was next and tried to outsmart her, but she caught his sudden shift, and before he realized what was happening, she yanked him off balance and flipped him to the floor.

"I'm truly sorry, David, but I can't let you examine my research."

David pulled himself up and dusted himself off. "We've done this before," he murmured.

She frowned. "What do you mean?"

He shook his head and walked toward her. He knew her weaknesses, and he was stronger, so he eventually had her back against the wall. "You *are* going to open the case. Simple as that."

He kept far enough to her side to believe he was safe from the zapping weapon he knew she carried, but he was wrong. He heard the clicking noise — agonizingly familiar — and fell to the ground, unable to move.

When he finally recovered a bit, his head was spinning. "The mini-taze?" He asked weakly.

"Yes. How did you know?" Her eyes widened. "You don't even have tasers yet. That's not until the '70s." She walked over and helped him to his feet, then guided him to the couch and sat him down. She stroked his head gently.

It felt good when she brushed the hair off his forehead. She brought him a glass of whiskey, then knelt in front of him and peered into his eyes. "Are you feeling better?"

He nodded, "Yes, much." He took a deep breath. "Miri, I don't understand what's going on, but there's something . . . something I can't explain. You need to be truthful with me."

"I'm not supposed to be interacting with anyone here. I should have never come to your cabin . . . but I was curious."

"Miri, this may be the ranting of a crazy man, but I am fairly certain that you are somehow from the future and that you have visited me previously."

She gasped and stared into his eyes. "I have?'

"Yes. You have. Are you from . . . from some time years from now?"

Sighing, she answered, "Yes."

"When?"

There was a long pause. "I'm not sure I should tell you."

"You can't *not* tell me. I keep secrets well. Besides" — he grimaced —"do you think anybody would believe me?"

She smiled. "I'm from the year 2165."

Chapter Twenty-one: It's a Pleasant Death

"I knew it. Somehow, I knew it, but I don't know how." David shook his head. "Hah, nice to know the human race makes it until 2165. Certainly surprising."

Miri chuckled. "It has been so hard keeping it from you. It's difficult not to be myself. I don't usually like to play-act." She gazed up at him. "And it has been especially hard to do that with you. You're so different from the men in my time."

"In what way?"

"Well, you're very sleek, like a cat. Your body is interesting. The men in my time are more like" — she laughed — "well, sort of like gorillas, in a large way."

He laughed, too. "I'm not sure that's a compliment. A cat compared to a gorilla?"

"It is." She smiled.

"What about the women?"

"We have more muscle."

"I suppose you do."

"Is it ugly? Am I a gorilla?"

"Not one bit."

"Would you like to compare bodies? You can look at mine, and I'll look at yours."

He cleared his throat. "Miri, people see each other's bodies when we care about each other . . . When we want to make love to each other. At least, that's how it is in my time."

"It's that way for us too, but we can look at each other without touching. It's natural to wonder."

"Instead of that, right now, there are a million things you could share with me."

She shook her head. "I've told you too much already. I was instructed, specifically, not to say anything to anybody. The only thing I was to do was get my samples and, if I needed to, protect myself. David, I can twist up time if I tell too much. I can twist up time with just the wrong words." She worried her bottom lip. "I can twist up time if I don't return when I'm supposed to. I can twist up my own future, my own body. If a woman doesn't return when she's supposed to, she can become infertile. Or if she already has children, those children can become sick or even disintegrate, and we can't afford that."

"Why? You don't have children. Do you?"

"Oh no, I've never been married, but I want children. We all want children. After the three big pandemics and the famines, we lost a lot of people. You said that it's nice the human race makes it until 2165. Well, there aren't a lot of us left."

"How many are left?"

"I've said enough. I don't want to scare you. Just know that we aren't brimming with people. I want to have children someday. After I get married, to be sure."

They continued to talk, but she skirted his questions about the future. Suddenly, the noise of the wind whipping around the cabin became so loud that it grabbed their attention away from their conversation.

"It sounds bad out there." Miri cringed.

"Yes, it does."

David walked over to the window and pulled the small curtain back. Miri joined him, and they both stared at the blizzard obliterating their entire view.

"I hope it stops by tomorrow," Miri commented. "I have to

get out there again."

"How many more days?"

"Three."

"Why are you collecting the water?"

She bit her lip. "I suppose I can tell you that." Miri explained how water collected by all the scouts like her would end up evaluated by the scientists in her time. They were attempting to remediate the ecological problems at the source. She turned serious. "And we know that's twisting time, but we're hoping to twist it in a positive way."

A little overwhelmed, David looked at her, "So, that's why the fear of plastics."

"It's not a fear, it's an abhorrence."

He nodded. "I think I need another whiskey."

"Me too." She got up and refilled both their glasses. "I'm getting used to these."

He chuckled and raised his glass. "Cheers."

"Cheers." She laughed. "That's an interesting toast, but a nice one."

They sipped their whiskey in momentary silence.

"I really like the way this feels." She stretched as she sat leaning against the back of the couch.

As David watched her, it was hard for him to think about anything except pulling her body to his, but he had to find out if there was more to her story than the little bit she'd told him. Many women were easily duped by people with nefarious purposes. He hoped that wasn't the case with Miri. That strange prescience he seemed to have about her said it wasn't, but he couldn't rely on *hocus-pocus*, it was his job to make sure.

He sighed. It was time to get to work.

He leaned back and smiled. "Isn't this better than blowing paper across the floor?"

She chuckled. "In a way. But don't think I'm letting you just do drinking. I've still got three more days and lots of game ideas." She raised her eyebrows and poked his leg.

"You're so cruel," he growled, then reached out and refilled their glasses. *Get rid of her inhibitions and loosen her tongue.*

He had done this lots of times and had advantages when it came to holding his liquor. Suddenly, he felt echoes inside him of this very scenario. Had he done this before with Miri? He was beginning to feel sure that everything with Miri had happened before, in another time or simultaneously, in some way he couldn't explain. And he suddenly felt a decaying in his spirit, as if this cheating, this sneaking, was already a betrayal.

Don't betray me this time, she had said in Stornoway. He wasn't the type to betray people—unless it was in service to his country. The job always came first. And that was why he was refilling her glass. He kept telling himself that.

"I'm going to get intoxicated," she objected and giggled, but she continued sipping. "Does it always feel this good?"

"Always." He leaned toward her. Her hair smelled just as he remembered. No, just as he expected—clean and a little like winter chestnuts. He might not feel right about doing this, but the scent of her was as intoxicating to him as the whiskey was to her. It was easy to bury his lips in that mass of hair. He heard her gasp as he dragged tiny kisses down her temple and felt the gentle pulse there. He let his breath linger over her ear, knowing the effect he was having on her. She pulled away slightly and looked up at him. He knew those eyes . . . intimately.

"That feels . . . And your face, it's so beautiful . . . Your eyes . . ." She pulled in a long breath. "How can anyone survive you?" Her voice was almost a whisper.

He grinned. "It's a pleasant death."

CHAPTER TWENTY-TWO: SO SWEET

She ran her finger up the side of his cheek. "I imagine it is a most pleasant death. You have a face like an angel. Your eyes have their own light. It must be like heaven . . . but so intimidating."

He gave her a mock frown. "Is that a compliment?"

"I think so." She cocked her head to the side and scrutinized him as if he were part of her water samples. "Amazing."

"I feel like I'm under a microscope." He cleared his throat.

"*His legs are as pillars of marble set upon sockets of fine gold,*" she began in a gentle voice. "*His countenance is as Lebanon, excellent as the cedars.*" She dragged a finger across his lips.

David smiled and stroked her face. "*Thy lips are like a thread of scarlet and thy speech is comely. Thy temples are like a piece of pomegranate within thy locks.* Sound familiar?"

"Song of Solomon. *Let him kiss me with the kisses of his mouth, for thy love is better than wine.*" She turned to her whiskey, blushing, and took another sip. "You are not under a microscope. You are up on a pedestal."

David was surprised to feel himself match her blush. This was why he had opened the Bible, why he had gone to that particular section. And why, after being absent from a church for many years, he had memorized those specific verses. He, too, turned to his whiskey glass, but instead of a sip, he took a big gulp. "So, they still have the Bible in 2165."

"Of course." And she explained how the people of her time respected religions and taught them."

"Of course, we have the World Belief, too."

"Which is?"

"We will put others' interests ahead of our own."

"And how exactly is *that* carried out?" He raised an eyebrow.

"By abiding with by the World Rules."

"What are the World Rules?" This was getting interesting.

She recited them, starting with *not harming anyone physically, emotionally, or materially* and ending with *seeking first to love then to be loved*. All of which sounded familiar to him.

"And if somebody breaks those rules?"

"They are gently reminded of them."

"What if they continue to break the rules?"

"That mostly happens with children but sometimes with adults. Then they are strangled-out."

She described how a mask was placed over the head of the offender. It included a section that wrapped around the person's neck to keep them from doing further harm, and their hands and feet would be bound. They'd sit that way until they were ready to ask forgiveness or at least comply. At the end of the day, they'd go home with gifts, knowing they are loved, whether they've asked forgiveness or not.

"And adults go home with gifts too?"

"Yes."

"And when it doesn't work?"

"The government has a place for those who don't comply, or if they must, they euthanize them. But that hasn't happened in decades. Not in my lifetime."

"What if you don't like rules?"

"There are some who live behind the mountains who don't like rules. Sometimes they even want to fight."

"I think I'd be like that. I'd be more of a freedom fighter."

"A freedom fighter?"

"Yes. I like freedom."

"And from which rule would you want freedom, David?

Putting others first? Listening before hearing, seeking to understand before being understood? Or would you want freedom from loving before being loved?"

"Well, one must do what they must do in order to protect themselves, their loved ones, and their country."

She nodded. "You are a product of your generation. Brash, like a little one. You haven't any idea of what it's like to accept pain without giving retaliation. You wanted to see my equipment, so you tried to force me. You believe in freedom for yourself and would fight for it, yet you pulled me by the hand, hoping to take my freedom from me." She smiled and drew her finger across his brow. "And now, look at you. Your mouth is like you are pouting, but your eyes are scowling. It does things to my heart. You make me want to hold you, to feel you, to have you as part of me."

Her cool touch against his hot forehead drained his heated intensity, and his tension melted. He had been waiting for this, and the knowledge that he longed for this moment stunned him. He knew this feeling, knew she would be soft, inviting, and he had missed her caresses. As he basked in her tenderness, he let what she'd said about World Rules sink in and began to wonder how that could work. No culture could really be like that. Humans were innately bad, weren't they? And to accept pain without retaliation? He could never do that. Could anyone do that?

She leaned forward and kissed his head. Soft rushes of excitement flowed through him. He wanted to lie back and have her kiss him all over, to receive love from her. It felt like he was always giving, giving, giving—giving pleasure because he needed to steal information. With Miri, he had known the sensation of letting go, of letting his mind drift, allowing her to kiss every inch of his naked skin, and he wanted that again.

He tried to shake the familiarity from his mind, but as she leaned over him, he could only bury himself further into her embrace, kissing her breasts through her sweater while she held him close. He had done this before, and somehow, he sensed a reflection of doing this elsewhere even now. He felt the intensity of twice the pleasure.

"You're so sweet," she whispered.

Only one person had ever called him sweet.

No—nobody had ever called him sweet. Only an echo of Miri, in some other time or in the distance. He felt drugged. Had she given him something, a new sedative? No, he was simply indulging himself in a moment of forgetting and reveling in the caresses of somebody he knew in his soul really cared about him. Someone who at one time had proven her care, but he wasn't sure how.

He breathed out a long sigh, then tucked himself more fully into her embrace. He hoped she was comfortable as he drifted blissfully into sleep.

Chapter Twenty-three: Fighting the Storm

David woke up to a chilled room. The fire was merely smoldering embers, and Miri was sound asleep. He extricated himself from her arms, then tucked a blanket around her. She snuggled under it, eyelids fluttering as she settled in. He ached to stroke her hair, to cling to her warmth, but he had to check in with Jensen. Flexing his fingers a few times, he forced himself to focus on the job at hand.

What was going on inside of him? As he peered down at Miri, he knew he loved her, had loved her for a long time. He had known her before now, before Stornoway, and felt as if they were fated to be together. His thoughts were in turmoil and disturbing. He couldn't ignore the possibility that he might have been detained, drugged, and brainwashed. Maybe given some sort of amnesiac pharmaceutical, then placed in this position purposely.

Yet deep in his gut, he felt this infernal bond, this unyielding connection, almost an obsession. An unremitting drive that compelled him to touch her, hold her, protect her, to see her smile and enclose her with his entire being. He felt all sorts of emotions he had never felt before, and yet *had* felt them before. These were feelings he did *not* want. They were of no use to him or to his purposes. They were feelings that had spun out of control and that he must constrain.

Somehow, he would regain control over himself, no matter how painful or difficult that task would be.

He crept into his bedroom and got on the radio with Jensen.

"She says she's from the future."

"The future?" Jensen's voice rose an octave.

"Year 2165."

"Well, our team is on the way. We'll get to the bottom of this."

"It may be true, Jensen. I don't know."

"What?"

"I'm serious. She has equipment, knowledge, answers to questions. But Jensen, they may be using some sort of mind control on me. I don't know." David felt catch in his throat.

"Okay. Take it easy, Morse. You'll both be debriefed. There is an immense amount of information we'd be able to extract from her if she is truly from 2165, but equally so if they have something strong enough to knock *you* off balance."

"Most assuredly. You'd be amazed at the technology she possesses — even a simple small weapon."

"A weapon, you say?" He sounded startled.

"Just a small one, for personal protection. But if our operatives had access to such things, it could be lifesaving. That's what got me wondering if she is genuinely from a different time. We have nothing like this."

"I'm looking forward to talking with this girl."

"So, when will you be here?"

"The team should be close to Barrow in a day, but that storm is sitting right over you, and we won't be able to get there until it lets up. We'll be stuck in Fairbanks or close by."

"Well, I'll keep getting what I can from her."

"Good job." Jensen paused and chuckled. "Are you using the Belgium Method? Must be fun if she's really from the future. I'll bet they have new ways to do it."

David had a hard time answering. "I don't like it, Jensen."

"Why? Is she ugly?"

"Not like that," he snapped. "It's just dirty work, that's all."

"Seems pretty pleasant to me. I'd be more than happy to take one for the team if I get a chance with her. Or I'll take more than one for the team. I'll take as many as she'll give me."

"Knock it off, Jensen. You're disgusting." David's jaw tightened.

"Since when did *you* get so sensitive?"

"I'm out."

Jensen laughed. "Okay, pal. Out."

David slammed the microphone on the hook then shoved the radio back into the wall. He looked over his shoulder to make sure he hadn't awakened Miri. He half wished she'd be standing there. Then he'd be forced to tell her the truth. Didn't she say she wasn't used to lying? Well, he was certainly used to it. And he clearly remembered her warning from Stornoway. She told him not to betray her.

The wind was whipping up outside, groaning and howling like the world was in pain, and the air was becoming bitterly cold in the cabin. He needed to get the fire going again. He had a job to do, and maybe Miri *was* actually plotting something. Perhaps *she* was going to betray *him*. He needed to focus on getting information from her — solid information — not just philosophical ideas from the future. Still, something inside of him was cracking, splitting . . . and it hurt.

Monday

David watched as Miri awakened and stretched in such a way that made him want to run his hands over her body. But he wasn't going to do that unless he needed to. *Yes, I am.* He knew he would, it felt inevitable. *No! Only for information.* He sat as far from her as he could in the small cabin.

"Breakfast?" he called out.

She stood, wearing only a thin pair of long underwear.

Hugging herself and shuddering, she looked out the window. "It's still storming. I can't see a thing." She rubbed the glass and bent to peer out. "I've got to get to the water." She started pacing, all muscles and flesh parading in front of him, gorgeous and agile.

"Miri, could you put some clothes on? There's not much to that long underwear." He shook his head to clear his lurid thoughts.

She looked down, seemingly unaware of how sheer her coverings were, then said, "Okay." In a few minutes, she emerged from the room wearing an outfit that outlined every curve.

David decided to pour himself a whiskey.

"Whiskey for breakfast?"

"I need it."

She gave him a puzzled look. "Is everything okay?"

He nodded.

"David, I've got to get to the water. What am I going to do?" She sounded frantic.

"You can't stay extra days, can you?" It was a rhetorical question, because he already knew the answer.

"I can't. I *told* you before. If I do that, I could become infertile, and I haven't had children yet." Her voice became slightly shrill. "Besides, I have no idea how I might twist up time if I stay longer than they have arranged for."

David went to the window and looked outside. "We don't have enough rope to get to the water." He wasn't anxious to face that blizzard. He had plenty of experiences hacking his way through extreme arctic weather, one strong man attached to another, fighting for each step as the expedition forged ahead, but he'd only done this once with a lone woman, and that had been nearly impossible. *No, not alone with a woman. What am I remembering?*

"Rope? I've got rope," Miri's answer broke into his thoughts. "Well, it's not exactly rope, but maybe even better than rope."

Miri ran to her room and returned with two good-sized spools of what she called perpetuline. David immediately knew in his gut that despite the fragile appearance of the line, it was completely unbreakable. And the spindles held lots of it. Enough for the trip to the water, with extra to spare.

Once they were geared up, David anchored the spindles to the cabin, then tied one each to himself and then Miri.

The air they walked out to was so blisteringly icy hat Miri was shivering in spite of her specially made outerwear. He dragged her forward as they fought the power of the storm. *All this for a couple cups of water.* He jolted slightly as a memory of this horrible experience chilled him as much as the reality of it. Nevertheless, he forged forward, putting one foot in front of another while dragging Miri along.

He had never done anything quite so grueling, except part of him was sure he had. He had done this exact same thing before, with Miri, right here, in this place. One wouldn't forget something this terrible.

He knew he had never physically done this in his lifetime, but he sensed a reflection of himself doing the same thing at the same time. As he took each step, another him was taking a step. He could *feel* it, he *knew* it, and the thought made him shiver even more than the cold.

After what seemed like hours, they reached the water. Miri fell to her knees and began her collections with shaking hands. Once the last cup had been sealed, she gathered her gear and stumbled to her feet, trembling convulsively. He grabbed her and tucked her inside his coat, holding her close to share his heat. He wrapped the fur tightly around them both and tucked his head close to hers. They stood like that until he believed she'd be able to make the walk back.

Once Miri's shivering had subsided, she slid out from his arms and nodded. David began the trudge holding on to her and the perpetuline to guide them through the blinding white. His steps quickened as he thought of the light and fire waiting back at the cabin.

CHAPTER TWENTY-FOUR: THIS IS LOVE

They were chilled to the bone and ravenous when they entered the cabin. David led them to the kitchen, where they wolfed down cans of refried beans without heating them. No words were spoken as they ate like beasts and drank several shots of whiskey.

Hunger assuaged, they moved closer to the fire and huddled together under a blanket. They each poked their cheeks and complained about the tingling and the burning, but they agreed it felt incredibly good not to be cold. Finally, they regained enough energy from the food and whiskey to really talk.

Miri frowned, and with a dejected tone, said, "I may have to go back without complete samples."

He nodded.

"That trek was truly horrible."

"It was," he agreed, then turned to her with a smirk. "I guess your jacket wasn't so good after all."

She bumped his shoulder with hers. "Maybe it was colder than negative fifty degrees out there." Then she shivered.

They drank a little more in silence, staring listlessly into the flames. David was tempted to relax and enjoy the peaceful moment, but he had a job to do.

He finally pulled back from the fire and leaned against the sofa. "Miri, tell me more about your world. What exactly is the World Government?"

"It's our government," she answered.

"What about countries?"

"Oh, we have countries, but a sparse population."

"Who governs the other countries?"

"It doesn't really matter." Miri shrugged. "I've never paid it much attention. I concentrated on my area of expertise, and I was chosen for this task because of it. With limited knowledge, it would be less likely for me to twist up time."

"So, children only study one area?"

"Well, they can study whatever areas they wish, but I was only interested in one."

David mulled that over. "Why water?"

"All ecological things are important, David. There were three pandemics. The first in 2020, which wiped out over five million people worldwide. It took a tremendous toll, but not really that big in terms of overall population density. Also, it mostly killed the elderly." Her eyes darkened. "Then there was the pandemic of 2089. That one hurt a lot more because it affected all ages and killed fifty-six billion people, about half the population of the world at the time."

"How did these pandemics start?"

"That has always been the question. Were they manmade or natural? Those questions led to mini-wars, which killed even more people. Then the famines began, which led to the deaths of even more. On top of everything else, we were struck with the impact of climate change and natural damage. Pretty soon, there weren't a lot of people left. So you weren't far off in suggesting that it was remarkable we made it until 2165 as a race. That's why the World Government was put into place, and that's why we adopted the rules very seriously. All the lower governments abide by the rules. It doesn't matter who or how, it only matters that we all care about each other, and we value every individual life. We use technical progression to save what we can."

He just stared at her.

"What I'm telling you is only part of it all. I couldn't even begin to explain the entirety of climate damage to you. That's what I study, but our whole mission here is to eventually place people back into appropriate eras and places to make a difference — without, of course, twisting time."

"And if you twist time?"

"That is not my specialty" — she shook her head — "but I know it would be terribly destructive. First to the person, then it could have much larger shock waves. Who knows? She raised a palm. "They have to figure out exactly how to go back and make tiny tweaks, enough to change the ecological course of the world." She took a sip of her whiskey. "My part is to bring back these samples."

"You need to tell me, are you doing anything else here? Anything at all?"

She laughed and shrugged, "That's it. That's all I can tell you. Ecology is my passion." She smiled up at him. "Ecology and dogs. I have a dog. Terra. T-e-r-r-a."

He snorted. "Mother Earth?"

"Yes," she chuckled. "You're well-read."

"Well, here's to Terra." He lifted his whiskey glass.

She clinked hers against his. "You know, I'm going to miss this when I go back."

"Just this?" He couldn't look at her, and his throat tightened. He was working his Belgium interrogation, but it didn't feel right.

She gazed up at him, and he finally looked back. She was beyond beautiful with the glow of the firelight across her face. "No, I will miss you, your eyes, your voice." She blushed and swallowed. "David, I need more of you. I need to touch you."

He studied her for a moment, feeling a flutter in his chest, then he set his glass down. He took hers and put it to the side as well. She reached for him, and he trailed kisses down her neck. He knew what to do. He knew how to excite a woman. He was a pro at this. Yet with her, it felt like a privilege, it felt wonderfully familiar. It felt like love.

He leaned his forehead against hers and felt her breath on his chin. It was tantalizing. He dragged his lips across hers, and the effects darted through him with a zing almost like the mini-taze. He pulled her closer, and his tongue joined hers, their mouths fully engaged. He reveled in the sound of her small moans and her responses to him.

The curve of her spine and the taut silkiness of her skin felt delightfully familiar as he lightly dragged his finger down her waist to her thigh. He knew what would happen next, and it took immense self-discipline to move slowly, but he kept a gentle pace.

When he finally felt the moment was right, he lifted her sweater and ran his fingernails along her exposed skin. He smiled at her trembling response. She yielded eagerly, as he knew she would, so he pulled the sweater up over her head. This time, he was completely aware of how to unclasp her bra, and he slid it from her shoulders. He drew a deep breath at the sight of her lovely familiar breasts, not caring anymore how he had become aware of so much about her. It was glorious to just bury his face in her flesh and inhale the scent he'd missed. He felt the vibrations of her moans as he nibbled and licked, and he gave her every pleasure he knew—and there were many.

Miri tugged at his shirt until he allowed her to slide it over his head. He leaned in to kiss her, and a groan ripped through him when her breasts pushed into his chest. The constriction of his slacks became unbearable, so he reached down to relieve the pressure, meeting her hand at his belt as they kissed. In silent agreement, they both stood and shed their clothes.

He held her away from him by her shoulders and just stood there, looking at her. "You"—his voice caught—"You, Miri, are so stunning." He swallowed to expel the threat of tears behind the pressure in his eyes. *What is this? What's going on with me?*

She frowned. "Are you okay, David?"

He merely nodded as he struggled to regain his composure.

"May I look at you?" Her quiet voice almost echoed in the silence of the cabin.

David relaxed and smiled. "Of course."

Miri gazed at him as she reached out, gently grazing his chest with her fingertips. She stepped to the side, eyeing his body and dragging her hands down his arms around to his back, then up to the nape of his neck. Now and then, she would kiss his exposed flesh, causing him to harden more than he thought possible.

A strange feeling nearly overwhelmed him, as if shadows of the two of them were doing this exact same thing at this exact same time on some other plane. He wrestled with the emotions elicited by her actions—a combination of excitement and a certain bashfulness. The echo created a double eroticism that was almost unbearable, the pleasure making it difficult to keep his spine straight. His body craved release, but he was determined to deny himself for as long as he could.

When she faced him again, her lips met his. He pulled her closer, savoring the feel of her breasts against him, her belly against his, and her body grinding against him. He kept a hand at the small of her back and drove the fingers of his other hand through her hair. He wanted to make this last. He was desperate to make it last. If she was really going to leave, he needed to memorize everything about her.

Finally, he pulled away and spread a blanket out in front of the fire. He coaxed her to the floor with kisses, then leaned over her to continue giving her pleasure, but she pushed his shoulders and gently forced him to his back.

He lay there while she rained kisses on his face, first his forehead, then down the angle of his cheeks. She kissed little circles around his mouth while he attempted to catch her lips.

She kissed his chin then moved up to his ears, sending chills through his body. But she didn't stop.

She trailed tiny kisses down his neck as he had done to her, then continued down his chest in a delightful zigzag pattern that made him moan when she reached his belly. Her lips passed near his most tender spots, and he arched his back with need. But again, she didn't stop. She continued her downward path, kissing every vulnerable inch of the inside of his left thigh, then lower and still lower to pay homage to his ankle.

He moaned and clutched the blanket. The pleasure was nearly unbearable, and his manhood throbbed in response. She then moved to his other leg and kissed her way up until she got to the crevice above his thigh. He could feel her breath on his waiting body. The anticipation drove him crazy. Then she wielded her soft, gentle touch, just slightly, before kissing and taking him into her mouth.

Sparks jumped through his head. He didn't care about anything, not the future, not the job, not the gear. His whole being was focused only on Miri and what she was doing to him. No woman had ever made him feel like this. No woman except Miri had ever cared to force him to lie back and enjoy. He was always the active one, giving pleasure and making sure the other was satisfied.

He wanted to move, to touch her, to participate, but every time he raised an arm or tried to sit up to join in, she gently pushed him down and compelled him to just enjoy. It was horrible . . . .and wonderful . . . and driving him out of his mind. He raised and lowered his body, breath coming faster and faster as her mouth became more insistent. Her fingers urged him on as well. All his muscles tensed, legs tightened, arms stretched as he tugged on the blanket, his head whipping from side to side. He opened his eyes slightly and looked down only to find her staring back. Their gazes locked, and the fire shooting through his body exploded. It was a sensation he had never experienced, and he never wanted it to stop, yet he could hardly bear the emotions. She climbed up next to him, and he held her. *This is love. This is love. Undeniable and real.* He gripped her more tightly.

No, it's not. You're just having some good sex. Don't get carried away. You're reacting like a dumbstruck teenager. But he didn't believe that, not at all. He just *wanted* to believe it.

CHAPTER TWENTY-FIVE: FIRST TIME

David stroked Miri's cool hair and kissed the top of her head. He reached down and began to draw small circles across the skin of her belly. Then he moved his fingertips closer and closer to her breast, and her gasp as he reached his target encouraged him to continue. His hands traveled over her smooth flesh as his breath whispered into her ear. His gentle caresses and patient attention weren't part of his job. He was supposed to get her into bed, do the deed, then get information during pillow talk, but he enjoyed this pure pleasure too much.

When she wrapped herself around him, he could tell she was ready for the next step. Still, he wanted to linger, to give her more. He explored her warmth, moving his fingers with deft skills. Miri's lips parted, and her eyes grew wide as she looked up at him.

"What?" Her question turned into a moan, then she writhed, and a scream caught in her throat.

David relentlessly kept her going. When he felt it was time, he pulled himself on top of her, and she welcomed him. Still, he was met with some resistance and a small gasp.

"Miri?" He stopped, suddenly realizing what he had missed all along. "You're a virgin, aren't you? This is your first time." He groaned and rolled away. He knew it . . . had sensed it.

"What's wrong?" She scooted on top of him, looking into his eyes with a hurt frown. "You don't want me because I'm a virgin?"

He turned away from her gaze. "Your first time shouldn't be like this."

"Like what?"

"With someone like me."

"But I want it to be you." She reached down and touched him. "I know all about sex. I learned about it and read about it, and I could have had other men. Many men have asked me." Her fingers teased him. "But I want it to be you."

He tried to pull away, but she held him down and began to kiss his chest, doing things she had done before, dragging her breasts across him. He was weak, unable to move.

"I've never done this, but I think I can make it nice for you. I can make it pleasant. I could do *this* more," she whispered as she moved down on him.

He was powerless against her onslaught and disgusted with himself. For a brief moment, he half-heartedly tried to push her away, but she persisted. He gave up, moaned, and pulled her to him, crushing his mouth against hers.

He didn't let up, bringing her to another peak. Finally, he lay her back and gently parted her legs. "This might hurt for a moment," he whispered and positioned himself.

She nodded and took a deep breath as he entered. She raised her hips to meet him, and he started moving slowly. Her eyes closed as he quickened the pace, feeling her pleasure grip him, encouraging him to push deeper and stronger.

His heart filled as he took her, feeling her body respond, watching her face, being wrapped in her love. He hated himself for what he was doing, but he loved her. He knew he loved her on every plane of existence. He would die for her if he had to. And with that thought, he exploded, knowing he was exploding in some other world at the same time, in the same position, in this same way. Then his mind lost all reason, lost all worry, lost all tension.

He lay in her arms afterward as he thought about their

lovemaking. Yes, it was lovemaking, not *sex*, there was a difference. He had never made love before. *Yes, I have, with Miri.*
Everything was so confusing. He was bonded to her. *No, get
that out of your head – unprofessional – you have a job to do.*

"David?" she whispered.

"Yes?"

"Is it always this good?"

"No, not always," he answered, but he thought it might
be . . . with her.

Miri began to drift off, still wrapped in David's arms, and
he wondered how he could ever do what he needed to do.
And how could any government have sent somebody like
Miri anywhere? She knew nothing about protecting herself.
Sure, she knew how to fight, she even had that weapon, but
she knew nothing about betrayal. She was totally unprepared
for a person like him, a sneak, a liar.

He stiffened, and Miri opened her eyes, gazing up at him.
He wouldn't look back. *She is going to learn about betrayal, isn't
she? She is going to learn about it from me.* He remembered again
what she had told him in Stornoway. *Don't betray me this time.*
Had there been another time? His throat tightened, and his
belly cramped as he became certain there had been.

Chapter Twenty-six: Whiskey in My Veins

He slid out from under the blanket, checking to see that Miri still slept. In the bedroom, he shivered a little as he pulled out the radio.

"Jensen," he kept his voice low.

"Go." Jensen's voice crackled through the speaker.

David turned the volume down. "Have you found out anything?"

"Nothing. Nothing at all." Jensen sounded baffled.

"I'm making headway."

"Good for you. Keep going with it, because there's a little problem."

"What problem?"

"Weather is still pretty bad there. You'll have to hold out a bit longer."

"Terrific."

"What's wrong? Do you think she's on to you?"

"No . . . No . . . It's just . . . it's . . ." He bit his lip. "I don't like this."

"What's not to like? Cabin bad? Food bad? Sex bad?"

"No, not exactly. It's just . . . I need a vacation."

"You'll get one, Morse, as soon as this is done."

"Yeah."

"Get what you can, and when we get there, we'll take her into custody."

"Yeah."

"Out."

"Out."

David pushed the radio back into its hiding place and sat silently. He lit a cigarette and then viciously stubbed it out. *I'm a professional – for the good of the free world.* He sighed, then went back to the living room and slid under the blanket with Miri. He had a job to do, but he had never been faced with a situation like this and had never before experienced such emotional turmoil.

Tuesday

Miri stepped out of the bathroom, fresh out of the shower, skin glistening and shivering.

"Come here, you look cold." David held out his arms, and she eagerly came to him. He pulled her over by the fire to warm her. "I know what you need."

He took off his clothes, grabbed his fur jacket and a thick blanket, then he sat down with the blanket wrapped over his shoulders. He leaned against the couch and patted his thighs. She laughed and climbed down in front of him with her back to his chest. He surrounded her with the blanket, then covered them both with his big fur jacket. Their legs, sticking out from underneath, glowed in the firelight, which flickered patterns across their flesh. He wrapped his arms in front of her and tucked his face close to the side of her head. If he could pull her into his own body and keep her there forever, he would gladly do so. He could not get enough of her, and she seemed to feel the same way. She melted into him, laying her head back and raising her breasts into his hands. He caressed them, stroking each one with his thumbs as she sighed.

"Are you warmed up now?" he whispered.

"Oh yes," she murmured.

He moved his hand down her belly, and she raised her hips, blatantly showing him where she wanted his touch.

"You want more?" he teased. "Maybe some more of this?" He caressed her delicately.

She gasped. "You make me feel . . ."

"Feel what?" he whispered.

"Something I've never felt before. Like there's whiskey in my veins." She turned to face him and climbed to her knees, bringing her arms out from under the blanket to wrap them around his shoulders. Her hands dug into his hair, and her lips grazed his face.

"You'll freeze like that," he whispered and stopped her. "I can already feel your goosebumps." With a chuckle, he ran his fingers across her breast. "Here." He gently moved her onto her back, snuggled her under the heavy fur, warm and cozy. Then he kissed his way down the curve of her body until he could bury his face in her soft flesh. His lips traveled over her belly, tasting her and taking his time. This was not part of the typical Belgium Method, but he couldn't keep himself from pleasuring her. He wanted to hear her cry out for him and needed to give all of himself to her, over and over again. He had felt this desire before — powerfully. *All of this has happened before.*

Although these thoughts spun through his head, he did not lose track of his enjoyment of Miri's body nor her reaction to what he was doing. She writhed under him, grasping his head and spouting encouragement, unlike other women, who had seemed almost ashamed of the joy they received from his attention. Her responses were uninhibited, with moans and whispers, begging him not to stop. She gasped and simply threw off the warmth of the jacket with her thrashing. The nip of the cold air hitting them only added to the thrill of the experience, and he scooted up and entered her in a single thrust.

She wrapped her legs around him, and he held her tight. Using all the strength he had, he moved into a kneeling position as she clung to him, keeping him inside. Every muscle tensed as he rocked her up and down. Her pleasure was evident by her body's reaction. As much as he wanted to prolong this joining, the ecstasy vibrating through him was overwhelming as he felt the reverberation of their passion in that otherworld.

When she reached her peak, he couldn't hold back. He clutched at her, once again knowing that this was more than something physical. This was a meshing of everything inside them, creating something that reached past time and space. That must be why he felt what he did.

Finally the peak ended, and he fell to the side, still clinging to her and landing on the fur. He reached out and gently slid his knuckles across her cheek, moving a stray lock of hair out of her face.

"Are you okay?" His voice sounded unusually tender, even to himself.

"I am more than okay, or maybe I'm not okay at all." She looked toward the ceiling, then back at him. "I am totally surrendered."

He gave a little laugh. "Don't say that."

Her eyes shone. "Oh, but I am. I am surrendered to you forever."

"No," he frowned.

She poked him gently. "You lied to me."

David's blood ran cold.

"I thought you said it didn't always feel this good." She smiled up at him.

He gave a little chuckle. "It doesn't. But isn't it more fun than games?"

"Yes, it's more fun than games, but you're still going to have to play games. We're not going out in that storm again."

"I think I'd rather go out in the storm than play more of your games." He made a face.

She pushed him, and they began a half-hearted wrestle.

"I could beat you," she laughed. "I almost did when we fought in the bedroom."

"You learned to fight in competitions, didn't you? In game competitions."

"Yes. How did you know? They're really fun."

"Well, you're good at it. Your people must be very competitive."

"Competitive? Oh, no. We just have fun. Nobody cares who wins. We just want to be better than we were the last time. We help each other improve. But games are fun."

"I don't understand."

"Well, I guess the games where I live are like what we just did. Just now, we each wanted to do more than the other, yet we wanted the other to succeed as well. It was sort of a competition, but we both won."

David laughed, "I guess we did."

"But what we did is more than that, isn't it?"

"In what way?"

"I feel this thing in my chest, like I want to give all of my being to you. It's strange. I would do anything for you."

He peered down at her. "Then, Miri, tell me what you are doing here. *Everything* you're doing. Is there anything about your research that doesn't have to do with water? Anything to do with governments or weapons?"

"No, just the samples." She sat up. "Do you think I plan to hurt you? To hurt your people?" Her eyes widened and began to brim with tears.

"No, I don't think *you'd* hurt us in any way." He put his hand to her face. "But maybe the others, the people you report to, maybe they have an agenda that you don't know about. It's happened before, and I wouldn't want you to get in any trouble because of them. I'm just trying to keep you safe— looking out for your best interests." *Is that what I'm doing?*

Miri pulled the blanket up in front of her. "My people don't hurt others. I told you that. But you don't believe me." She bit her lip. "David, I want you to trust me. Your mistrust hurts my insides. Will you feel better if I let you look through my things? You just cannot touch the samples, okay?"

He nodded.

"I don't understand why this is so important to you or why you have this mistrust, but it hurts knowing you think I could do you harm."

He quickly got dressed. It didn't escape his notice that she remained vulnerable, simply wrapping the blanket around herself and following him into her room.

She snapped open the kit, revealing neat rows of water cups, the dipsticks he had seen her use, what was left of the perpetuline spindles, and the cutting device used on the line. He spotted a small item he identified as another mini-taze and a few other things he hadn't seen before.

"What's this?" he asked, holding up a cube-shaped item.

"That's what I will use to go back through the portal. It's sort of a key."

David placed it back in the box and went through the rest of the items. Everything seemed innocent—powdered food she would have eaten had she not been with him, an object to melt snow into potable water, and other incidentals.

He shook his head. "Put your kit away."

"You're not afraid of me now, are you? Or my people?" She looked at him with hopeful innocence.

He nodded. Her glowing smile gave him a dull ache, but he forced his lips to curve. "How about one of those games?" he asked.

"What's wrong?" She frowned.

He cleared his throat. "I . . . I just feel bad for being so suspicious."

"Oh . . . no," she came over and hugged him. "No, don't feel bad for anything with me." She stroked his hair. "I will show you whatever you want, explain whatever you need. You are beloved always," she whispered and held him tight.

His tension eased, as if she could draw away all his troubles with just a touch, but he knew that *he* was trouble for her. Still, he nestled against her for a moment. "Miri." His arms raised and encircled her. "I'm sorry."

"Shhh," she stopped him from saying more and just held him.

Chapter Twenty-seven: For All Time

Later, David gave in to playing Miri's games. In spite of the heaviness in the pit of his stomach, he found himself laughing and behaving like a teenager. As the afternoon faded toward evening, he dropped onto the couch. "The storm is dying down."

"Well, that's good." She sat beside him.

"I don't think I could stand another day of your crazy games." He smiled, swallowing as he gazed at her.

"I'll never stop!" she cried, then jumped up and straddled his lap, facing him. Putting her hands on his shoulders, forcing his back against the couch, she continued. "You are mine, to do with as I please." She held his face, pushed her lips against his, and pushed her tongue into his mouth.

"Miri." He pulled away from her. "We can't do this." He had gotten all the information he could get from her. She had let him see the equipment. There was no reason to continue the Belgium stuff, no more interrogation needed.

"Oh, no?" she said with a smirk.

Her hips began to undulate, and his body instantly rose to meet hers.

"We can't," he murmured.

"It feels like you *can*." She laughed and redoubled her efforts. "I'll bet you can." She reached down and began to undo his pants.

He lost the battle. The scent of her hair, the feel of her fingers on him, the pull of his heart, combined with the echoes from another world, were impossible to ignore, despite his usual self-discipline. This situation was completely out of his control. He was saturated in layers and layers of Miri. He didn't know how it all worked or how it happened, he only knew he was completely helpless against her.

"I can't get enough of you," she whispered.

He dragged her to her feet and tore at her clothes. She pulled his shirt from him, and before long, they lay naked, breathing so hard the sound echoed in the room.

"Slow down," he murmured.

She nodded, and they lay side by side, staring into each other's eyes for endless moments. Finally he began kissing her. He held her face with his palms, tilting it ever so slightly, making sure to slide his lips over every inch. He lingered on the pulse at her temple, breathing in the fragrance of her skin. His own pulse quickened as he felt her fingers creep down his belly and find their target.

"I want to make love to you, Miri," he whispered in her ear. "I want to keep you here with me forever."

She looked up at him. "I wish I could stay." Tears blossomed. "But you know I can't."

He nodded and swallowed, then he pulled her on top of him and joined his body to hers, gazes still locked. He felt himself drowning in her, going under, not even able to breathe.

She clutched him and moaned, "I love you, David. I love you." She rose and gasped as her entire body drew him in.

He gave way to her and answered, "I love you too, Miri. I have always loved you." He didn't care. For one resonating moment, he just didn't care about anything but her. He loved her. He loved her now. He loved her then, whenever then was. And he believed he would love her for all time. He had to have her, and he held onto her with every confidence that what he felt was real. He was giving himself to her in the deepest ways he could and somehow knew he was doing the same thing simultaneously on some other plane. How his heart could bear the swelling of this double love, he wasn't sure. As a matter of fact, he thought it might very well kill him, but that didn't matter. The only thing that mattered was loving her.

When they finished making love, he clung to her, almost afraid to speak. Here she was, in his grasp, a woman whom he undoubtedly loved but who also had equipment and knowledge that could greatly benefit his government. If he did not turn her over to the authorities, he would be betraying his country. But if he did, it would be the most horrendous betrayal of his life, so horrific that it had caused her to step further back from the future and warn him in Stornoway. *But why?* Why shouldn't she stay here, in his time? If she never went back to 2165, she could stay with him. The government would give her accommodations. He and Miri could stay together right now. She could be his wife. If she understood the importance of her staying here with him, she would get over his betrayal. She'd be glad to stay, wouldn't she?

She pulled him from his musing when she reached up and stroked his hair.

"I love the way your hair curls when it's wet." Her eyes sparkled as she looked at him. "I love you, David."

He smiled down at her. "I love you so very much, Miri."

She smiled sadly. "But, David . . ."

"Yes?" He worried at the seriousness in her voice.

"We have so little time. I have to leave tomorrow, by the end of the day."

"Tomorrow?" He sat up, frowning.

She sat up, too, and nodded. "I have to go tomorrow. If I don't, I'll begin twisting time."

"Are you sure?"

She nodded.

"How do you leave?"

"I go to the portal. It's about a mile away." She moved closer to him, her breast brushing his arm. "If I could stay, I would. If it were just me, I would give up my life there to stay with you. But it's much bigger than either of us." She frowned.

David reached out and pulled her to his chest, and they sat in silence while he stroked her hair. Every part of his heart hurt.

She slept soundly, innocently, as he crept to his room and dragged out the radio.

"Morse! What happened? I thought the girl did you in. You okay?" Jensen's voice boomed loudly.

David cringed, wondering if the noise had awakened Miri. "Jensen, keep your voice down?" He adjusted the volume.

"Sorry. So what's going on with the girl?"

"She's due to return tomorrow. There's nothing else we can get from her. I've gotten all there is."

"I doubt that. You must be losing your touch. You said she's due to go back tomorrow?"

"Yes. Jensen, I said *there's nothing more to get.*"

"Well, we'll find out soon enough. The storm's ending, and we'll be at your front door mid-morning."

"You don't need her. I'll fill you in on everything."

"Morse, if she's really from 2165, there's a wealth of technical knowledge she can give us. Her equipment can be studied by our scientists. And we've got a doctor lined up. He's going to examine her body structure, inside and out. He'll be able to evaluate how people evolve in the coming centuries." Jensen snorted. "How can you possibly say there's nothing to get?"

David's fists tightened at the thought of Miri's body being coldly studied. And what did he mean by *inside*? "She's not going to share anything. She's been given strict instructions by her superiors."

"Morse, she'll share whatever we want her to share. We'll make sure of that. We have our ways. For God's sake, what's wrong with you?"

David was silent.

"You've done a great job. After we pick her up tomorrow, you'll be debriefed then off you go on vacation. I've even arranged for an air force jet to fly you home. Well, as close to home as possible. Then you can pack your bags and get ready to lie on the beach. I think you need it. You seem edgy."

"Yeah, out."

"Out."

David put away the radio and sat for a while with his hands on his head. Finally, he stole back into the living room. Miri lay sleeping serenely with one leg thrust out from under the blanket and one breast exposed. He knew all along it would come to this, and he didn't like it one bit.

He needed some water. No, he needed some whiskey. He clenched his fists and headed to the kitchen.

CHAPTER TWENTY-EIGHT: BETRAYAL

Wednesday

David sat in a kitchen chair, where he'd been all night, watching over Miri and dreading what he knew was going to happen this day. When she awoke, he forced a tight smile. "Get up, Miri. Get your things together."

She frowned and walked slowly to the bedroom, "Okay." She glanced back at him before she disappeared.

Once the door was closed, David took a deep breath and decided to make her something to eat. It wasn't long before she came back out, dressed and packed.

"I don't have to go until tonight, David. I was hoping—"

"Don't hope." He took a breath, forcing an air of indifference.

"I don't understand."

"Here, have some breakfast." He shoved a plate at her.

She sat and ate for a few minutes, then her fork clattered to the table. "Can you talk to me about this?"

"Nothing to talk about."

"David," she reached out to him.

He pulled away, certain her touch would crumble his control, then he walked over to the window.

She spun in her seat to face him. "David, what's going on?"

Suddenly, motors roared outside the cabin, and Miri stood up. In moments, the door burst open, and four men in riot gear entered, raising guns. Miri's eyes widened as she looked from David to the men and back to him.

"Come with us, ma'am," one of the men ordered.

Miri's gaze held questions and fear, and she reached out to David. "David?"

The men moved forward, and two of them took her by the arms. The other two patted her down.

"No weapons," one of them announced. "She's clear."

"Okay, get her in the APC," another said.

She cried out when they began to pull her away. "David!"

At that moment, Jensen entered the cabin. "Great job, Morse." He winked and slapped David on the back and peered at Miri. "Looks like you had a good time here. Cozy place. Belgium Method must've been fun. We'll debrief you, then you can be on your way."

Miri's eyes misted up, and her jaw dropped slightly. "David?" she said one more time in a quiet questioning tone.

He looked over at her, struggling to keep his expression impassive as his throat tightened, "It's a job, Miri. I don't necessarily like it."

Her knees gave way, and the two soldiers half-dragged, half-carried her out of the cabin. A third toted her equipment while a fourth gathered her things from the shed.

"Someone will need to return the snowmobile," David managed through gritted teeth.

Jensen nodded and waved down a soldier to take care of it. David climbed into Jensen's oversized vehicle for the ride to Barrow.

"What now?" David asked although he was almost certain he knew the answer.

"We'll debrief you and begin our interrogation of the girl. We'll need a report of everything she told you." Jensen glanced at him. "It must have been fascinating. Are you sure it's true?"

"Yes."

"Amazing." Jensen shook his head. "I'm anxious to get

started on her. All top secret, of course. Those boys out there have no idea how big this is or who they've got in custody." He turned back to David. "So, Morse, you'll finally be off on vacation after this. How long has it been?"

"Four years."

"Yeah, been three for me. Tough on guys like us. The others are right, though. They say you're one of the best."

"Do they?"

"Sure do. They've made a legend of you." He chuckled. "You'd better be careful."

"I'm hardly legend material." David turned and looked out the window. "So where is it that we're going?"

"Underground bunker in Barrow. Tight security—unknown to both friend and foe. After that, we'll get her on a plane to London, then maybe DC. She'll make the rounds before we're finally finished with her."

"And when will that be?"

"Who knows?" Jensen shrugged. "Once this breaks, there'll be a whole list of people who'll want to see her, talk to her, get information from her."

David looked down at his fur gloves clenched into tight fists. He blinked when he noticed a foggy shadow, like a double-exposed film. A clear reminder that this was not the first time he had seen this view, and he knew what he had to do. "Stop the car, Jensen."

"What do you mean, stop the car?"

"Just stop the car."

"Why?" Even as he asked, Jensen ordered the driver to pull over then radioed the rest of the small convoy to do the same.

"The girl can't ride in that APC. She needs to ride in here with us." David's mind worked a mile a minute. "And her equipment too."

"But, Morse, the APC will keep her contained." A frown formed between Jensen's brows. "I don't understand."

"No, you don't. You didn't just spend five days with her. She's clever. We need her right here. She needs to stay within my sight until we get to the bunker. If we don't do that, odds are we'll find a couple of knocked-out soldiers and an empty APC when we get there.

"Okay, Morse, whatever you say." Jensen gave him a sideways glance.

"Just get her and all of her equipment into this vehicle and send the others on ahead. We'll do this alone." David ignored Jensen's questioning look and waited for him to move.

Jensen paused, then nodded and stepped out to give the orders. A couple of soldiers loaded Miri's kit, tent, and cart into the back of the large vehicle. David kept his focus on Miri as she staggered forward between two hulking uniformed men. They helped her up into the seat across from David, where she sat trembling, hands cuffed behind her back.

"Uncuff her," David ordered.

They reluctantly did so. Jensen joined them shortly thereafter.

"Send the others ahead," David repeated. "We'll ride with her alone." Then he reached over to make sure the sound-proof partition was closed between them and the driver.

David watched the rear lights of the other vehicles disappear into the mist, then sat for a few more minutes in silence. He could hear Miri's breath come out in little shivers. There was no doubt she was terrified, and he hated himself for not taking her to the portal before the team had arrived.

"Look, Jensen, she's got to go back."

"What?"

"She's got to go back today. If she doesn't, there will be terrible repercussions."

"She's not going back, Morse. There's too much we can learn from her. Even *you* mentioned a weapon that we could use."

David shook his head. "You don't understand, Jensen. We're playing with time here. The repercussions are beyond our understanding. She's got to go back."

"I don't think so." Jensen looked over at Miri, who sat quietly, head down, hair quivering as she shook. He seemed less convicted as he watched her.

"I'm sorry, Jensen." In a flash, David grabbed Jensen's pistol from his holster and pointed it at the man. "We take her back with your help, or we go back in such a way that I wake up with a court-martial tomorrow."

Jensen glanced down at David's hand. "You believe in this that much, huh?"

He nodded.

"You realize this could ruin your life, Morse? You could spend the rest of your days in a penitentiary."

"I know that, but it's better than ruining the future."

"Okay, we'll go back." Jensen shrugged his shoulders. "I can't argue with *that*." He nodded down toward the gun. "Where are we going?"

"Give him the coordinates, Miri."

She choked them out, and Jensen passed them on to the driver.

As they headed to the portal, Jensen turned to Miri. "So, you're really from 2165 then?"

She nodded.

His eyes filled with awe. "Can you tell me anything about it?"

She gave a shaky smile. "It's peaceful. We have no need for guns or armies or wars. We want the earth to be healthier. That's why I am here. And I just want to go home." A tear ran down her cheek, and she wiped it off with the back of her hand. "It's so frightening in your time."

David's heart cringed. He wanted to reach out and hold her, but he knew Jensen would never understand.

When they got near their destination, David tapped on the partition and instructed the driver to stop. David helped Miri out while Jensen unloaded her gear. They left the driver sitting in the vehicle as they walked around behind an overhang, then headed for the portal area. Miri pulled her key from the kit, and the three of them carried her things in the direction she needed to go.

Finally, she stopped and turned. "David?"

He swallowed hard. "Miri."

"David, I love you."

"How? How could you?"

"It's easy."

He reached out and grabbed her, holding her so tightly he was afraid she wouldn't be able to breathe.

"David? Do you have a picture? I know I shouldn't . . . but do you have a picture I can take back with me?"

He dug in his pocket. In his wallet were the two identical photos of himself and his mother. He grabbed the one she had brought to him in Stornoway.

"Here. This is me with my mother." He pressed it into her hand.

She reached up to stroke his hair, then she kissed him before moving toward an open space. She smiled, then twisted the cube, and he watched her flicker and fade, his gaze locked on hers.

David stepped back and stood by Jensen, staring at the spot where she'd disappeared. All that remained was a bit of melted snow where she had just been standing. After a few silent moments, he and Jensen headed back toward the car.

David handed the gun to Jensen. "Would you like to handcuff me now?"

"Don't be ridiculous."

David turned toward him.

"I'm not taking you out of service for *this*." Jensen shook his head. "What if you're right, and we had put things in jeopardy by changing the course of time?" He kept walking. "We'll just make something up for the report."

They got in the car. "Nobody knew the details of why she was being transported. Nobody will ever know." He snorted. "Hah, they probably wouldn't believe us if we even tried to report it. How could I court-martial you?"

David smiled, then turned and looked out the window, watching the white landscape as they drove. His heart felt a relieved gladness even as an intense sorrow rose in his throat. One thing was certain. He would never use the Belgium Method again.

PART IV—NOVEMBER 1970

CHAPTER TWENTY-NINE: A PACKAGE

David Fitzpatrick, formerly known as David Morse, currently traveled under yet another moniker of the many he possessed. He had just finished up a month-long assignment in Bulgaria and was exhausted. He fumbled with his keys and finally stumbled into his flat.

It had been three long years since he had come back from his brief vacation in the Mediterranean. Once he'd returned, they had put him right back out again, and he'd had no time off since. But that was fine, he wanted to keep busy. The whole girl-from-the-future business continued to haunt him even now. He had fallen and fallen hard. He feared he would never feel anything for another woman.

And maybe that was just as well. Having a woman in his life was trouble anyway.

His problem now was that Jensen wouldn't get it through his head that there would be no more *Belgium Method*—ever. David was through with that. He'd never liked it in the first place. In Belgium, it was meant to be a one-time deal to get information desperately needed. After a repeat in Lithuania, he had begun to feel like a male whore. Jensen had just laughed it off and thought of it as David *getting lucky*. Jensen had no ethics or compassion for any of the women. Still, until Miri, David had kept doing as Jensen advised. After seeing what Miri had gone through, he had sworn never to use the method again.

David threw his suitcase on the bed and loosened his tie, then he went to get a glass of water. Cynthia, the lady that tidied his house, had brought in the mail. She had left the envelopes stacked neatly on the table. One large brown one, however, stood out from the rest. He picked it up as he sipped. *No return address. Odd.*

He set down the glass and tore open the envelope. Inside was a letter and some pictures of a small girl with tousled hair. He unfolded the letter and started reading.

Dear David,

One of our people is delivering this to you. They have allowed me to explain things. For me, it has been six years since we met at Snow Owl, but I know it has only been three years for you.

After I left you the first time, the time when you betrayed me, I was late returning home. When I went back to my era, everything seemed fine. The doctors checked me, and I was well. There appeared to be no repercussions for me, my time, or yours, but then they discovered I was carrying your child.

David's hand tightened on the paper, and he glanced at the photos. *My child?* He fought back his tears and resumed reading the letter.

Our baby is the first-ever across-time baby, and of course, everyone was excited. There were some who were horrified and upset and others who were fascinated. But mainly, all of them worked together to make sure my health was well and that the baby could be born successfully, allowing me to give her a happy, full life yet having her carefully evaluated for issues or conditions due to her unique circumstances.

Things went well with her at first. She was such a fun and happy baby and grew into a beautiful, smart, curious child. But then, when she reached the age of five, she began to wane. She started to disintegrate. She would flicker and fade. It was terrifying. I was losing her, just like the women who stayed too long on the other side had lost their children. Of course, our baby was the first intra-era baby.

The whole scientific world was in as much of a frenzy as I was, so it was determined that we should attempt to gently twist time and see if that would save her.

I felt badly for the mothers who had lost children and weren't extended this opportunity, but in our community, we give joy to those who receive even what we don't have, and they encouraged me.

I worked with the astrophysicists, the physiologists, and other specialists, and they directed me to visit you in Stornoway, where they delivered an explosive they felt certain would draw you. It caused no injuries but created a mystery that surely would attract a young, dynamic operative. And they were correct. I couldn't tell you too much, or time might have been twisted beyond repair. If you knew too many details, you might have been awaiting me in 1967 with scientists and the military. But I could carefully warn you in general terms that we would meet again and that I must return to my time as scheduled. That was all. I had hoped the photo of you with your mother would convince you of my legitimacy.

Then came our second time around. Because of the twist, I could not relive it. I had to actually go back without knowledge of the first time. That's why I didn't know you. You, however, were reliving it, otherwise, you might have betrayed me a second time.

You, David, you were the twist. We just prayed that you would be okay, and you were. But I knew in my heart if you realized you were doing it for our little girl, you would have been glad to risk anything.

There was one repercussion, though. Because you were the one to relive it, the time twist caused a split. Another one of you was somehow created. That means, David, there is a copy of you out there somewhere. He is identical to you. He may not have your same job or even your exact history, but his tendencies will be very similar to yours, and you will look exactly alike. He has your DNA. I believe you are aware of what that means.

Because of this split and the DNA copy of you (who is even now out there in your time), the people of my time have allowed me to ask you to join me here in 2171. There are not a lot of us, so having another is good. And this way you can be the father of your child.

We can be together and maybe have more children if that's what you wish.

If it is — if this is something you desire, then please be at our portal (the one where you left me) on December 4th at 1500 hours. I will wait for you but can only leave it open until 1700 hours.

I will understand if you do not want to leave your life in your time and will not try to seek you out. But I love you with everything I am and hope you will choose to be with your daughter and me. I will make your life here as wonderful as I possibly can.

Love,
Miri.

David's heart moved from sheer shock to sheer joy. He barely recognized such happiness, it had been so long since he had felt anything close to it. Of course, he was going to go to Miri. He didn't care what the future would hold. If he had to learn to shut up and listen to other people, he could do it. He could stop acting like a child. He chuckled to himself. He could even take pain without retaliation. Oh yes, he remembered the World Rules very well.

He rushed around deciding what he'd have to take — almost nothing — and what he could leave behind — almost everything. He glanced at the calendar hanging in his kitchen. He had three weeks to go, enough time to prepare.

Finally, he sat and examined the photos of his new daughter. She was remarkable, beautiful. She had his eyes, he could see that, and his mouth, but she had Miri's hair, except it was full of curls like his.

This was a dream . . . a miraculous dream.

CHAPTER THIRTY: RESIGNATION

A week later, David drove to Jensen's office and parked down in the garage. He'd planned to merely tender his resignation, but he still burned with anger about the whole Belgium Method issue and several other ethical breaches that enraged him. When he reached Jensen's office, he ended up delivering an entire tirade, then slammed his resignation down on Jensen's desk.

Jensen had stayed silent while David ranted, then finally looked up at him and asked, "Are you finished?"

"Yes," David took a breath.

"In this business, David, you know you can't resign."

"Watch me."

"You either get killed in the line of duty, or you wait until you're too old to function, then retire. Those are the only two ways you get out of it. You know that." Jensen shook his head. "Now take this back, go home, and get some rest. Maybe you just need another vacation." Jensen picked up the envelope and held it out.

David waved it away. "I *am* resigning, Jensen." He drew in a long breath. "Don't get me wrong, I know I let my temper get away with me there for a few minutes, but I am resigning. I'm leaving the country."

Jensen let out a heavy sigh. "David, do you know what they'll do to you if you resign and leave the country? Do you know what they'll think?"

"I don't care what they think." David turned toward the door.

"Do you remember Adamson?"

"Yes." David looked back over his shoulder. "He left five years ago."

"Have you seen him since?"

David thought for a moment. "No. Why?"

"You haven't seen him since because he can't be found."

"What are you saying, Jensen?"

"David, when people resign and tell us they're leaving the country, that is extremely suspicious."

"You know it's not like that for me. There is nothing to be suspicious of."

"I may know that, but the powers that be . . ." Jensen offered up the envelope again. "Take a vacation, David."

"Fine." David walked back toward Jensen and snatched the envelope from him. "I'm on vacation—for the next month—and I'm leaving the country."

"Where are you going?"

"Alaska."

"Alaska?" Jensen raised his eyebrows.

"Yes, Alaska."

"Suit yourself—Alaska in November." Jensen dismissed him and picked up his phone.

David left without another word.

CHAPTER THIRTY-ONE: TWIST

John Davidson, an American operative currently traveling to the frozen tundra of the north, carried several passports with him. Sometimes he traveled as John Peterson, sometimes as Thomas Morrison, sometimes as Thomas Hartman, and numerous other monikers. He was tired out from his last mission and looking forward to the long flight ahead of him.

He had been assigned a rather interesting mission. A British operative had been conducting himself in a suspicious manner. After years of crackerjack performance, the man had first threatened to resign, then when talked out of it, left the country to take a supposed vacation in Alaska during the dead of winter.

Alaska was suspiciously close to Russia. The powers that be, of course, were quite convinced that the operative was going over to the other side. This guy had way too much information for that to be allowed. John was to keep an eye on the guy, watch for the meeting, then detain both the operative and the connection. Of course, the traitor would be returned to Britain for court-martial, but the Russian would be dealt with on American soil. A win for both countries involved.

John stretched out his long legs and attempted to cover up with the scrap of a blanket a young Airman had given him earlier. *I could do with a double shot of brandy right now. That would give me more warmth than this thing.* He pulled out a cigarette and finally got a chance to break the seal on the file they'd delivered before he boarded the plane.

He flipped it open and immediately struggled to gain control of himself before he dropped the lit cigarette in his lap. There, staring up at him, was a photo of himself.

He must have gotten a wrong file, or somebody had slid his photo in there accidentally, since John was assigned to this job. John perused the fact sheet. The guy was the same height, weight, blood type, smoked the same brand of cigarettes, and drank the same alcohol—to excess, just like him. The imprint on the photo told him that this was indeed the operative known as *David Morse*, along with a dozen other monikers. They could have been twins.

Maybe they were twins, separated at birth somehow, but John found it difficult to believe that his provincial mother would have had any kind of history like that. Whatever the case, he was certain he had been put on this job purposely.

Various notes were deleted from the file, notes having to do with Morse's last trip to Barrow. It would have been nice to know what *that* was all about. He felt as if he hadn't been given the full story intentionally, yet he was being cast into a position that held a great deal of potential danger. This man knew how to kill, had been in this business as long as John, and had done things that were as devious and clever as anything John could think up. The guy had friends on both sides of the border, could shoot with his left and right hands, and for all John knew, could probably shoot blindfolded, too, for crying out loud.

He shook his head as he read. This was not a good situation, especially not if he wasn't given every detail. Did they think that a man like Morse was just going to meet up with a Russian operative right out in the sunshine? Although, there wasn't any sunshine up in Alaska right now. And did they expect John to be able to handle both Morse and a Russian operative single-handedly?

No. No, they didn't. It slowly dawned on John that they expected him to do away with Morse and take his place for the meeting with the Russian. That was the only thing he could think of. They didn't say it explicitly, but they knew that when John saw Morse's picture, he'd figure it out for himself. They wanted him to kill his lookalike and take his place. He let out a long breath.

Well, he'd do what he had to do. It wouldn't be the first time he'd taken on a difficult task. He'd done worse. Morse should have realized that you can't betray your country, especially if you're in *this* business.

CHAPTER THIRTY-TWO: MEMORIES

David got to Barrow on December 2nd. He had worried about cutting it too close, but nobody would be at Snow Owl this time of the year, so he figured he could go there a couple days in advance and wait it out. Then, even if it stormed, he would make it to the portal. He had plotted out the coordinates so that he could find the path no matter what, he'd make sure of it. To that end, he had stocked up on rope.

He rented a snowmobile in Barrow and let the rental people know where he was going. They looked at him as if he was crazy, but he wanted them to be able to get the vehicle back when he didn't return. No reason for them to suffer the loss just because he was stepping a couple centuries into the future. He chuckled at the thought.

The Snow Owl keys were exactly where they had been previously, and he soon had the generator going and a fire blazing. Being in the cabin ignited memories of Miri. They seemed so vivid that his anticipation heightened with an edge of desire. The feel of her and the scent of her wafted through his mind as he sat, eyes closed, sipping whiskey and daydreaming. It was hard to sleep that night. He was cold and lonely and unbearably excited.

Upon awakening, he couldn't tell if it was day or night, it was simply dark. Only by lifting his wrist and looking at the illuminated hands on his watch was he able to figure out that it was time to have breakfast. *December 3rd, just make it through today.*

He pulled himself out of bed and dragged himself into the kitchen. The can opener was still in the top left-hand drawer, and he smiled, remembering the day he showed Miri how to use it. *What will her can-opener be like? How will her kitchen look? What sort of fabulous things will I see in the future?*

The enormous possibilities overwhelmed him. Cars that drove themselves, people that didn't fight, could that all be real? *And I'll have to remember to shut up and stay out of trouble when I get there. I do not want to be strangled-out, that's for sure.* He imagined Miri giving him one of her looks, maybe gently tapping his hand if he got out of line. He bet she was a wonderful mother – she certainly was a delightful woman. And she was soon to be all his.

Throughout the day, he kept himself busy stoking the fire and dreaming about the future. His future, their future, the little girl that waited to call him *Daddy*, and the mysteries of the place he was going to. The thoughts assaulted his imagination, and there were moments when all he could do was pace around the small cabin, thinking about the possibilities. He was grateful when evening rolled around. *By end of day, tomorrow, I'll be with Miri.*

As he twisted open a can of spam, he heard a motor in the distance. *Odd, and not good. Nobody should be out here this time of year. This has to be trouble coming my way.*

He reached for his pistol and tucked it behind his back. He placed another gun in the can opener drawer, leaving the drawer slightly open. He stood poised, listening to the motor stop and the crunch of footsteps through the frozen snow. The doorknob jiggled. Then there was a knock. David stayed quiet, but the knock came again.

"Listen, I know you're in there." The voice coming from outside sounded familiar but spoke with an American accent. "Let me in, Morse. We have to talk."

David crept over to the side of the door and opened it slowly, using the door as a barrier against the other man, then cocked his gun. The stranger spun around but couldn't quite reach David, since David had taken a step back rather than putting the gun to the other man's head. When the stranger turned to lunge at him, David used the man's momentum to knock him off balance and pin him face-down to the cabin floor, then he shoved his weapon against the back of the man's head.

"Okay," David said, "push your weapons out and away from you."

The man pushed a gun out and slid it across the floor.

"And what else?" David waited. "I know you have at least a knife and probably another gun. Don't make this difficult."

Another gun came sliding out, then the man reached down into his left boot and pulled out a knife. He slid that across the floor as well.

"Now, roll over—slowly."

The man rolled to his side then onto his back. David was stunned but not so shocked that he gave his lookalike any leeway to attack. He had known this man was out there someplace and wasn't terribly surprised the guy ended up here.

"So, you're an American?" David stood and swung the gun up a few times, indicating the other man should rise. "What's your name?"

"John—John Davidson—at least right now." A familiar crooked grin spread across his face.

"Good god, you *do* have my DNA. She was right about the twist."

"What are you talking about?" The blue in John's eyes darkened as a frown formed between his brows.

"Go sit down," David waved the gun again, pointing toward the couch. "I've been doing this longer than you."

"Possibly." John's voice wavered slightly. "I've been in the business for a number of years."

"Right," David smirked. "A number of years—about

three?"

John's frown deepened as he plunked himself down. "I've been in the business for about a decade and a half."

"I'm sure you have." David sat across from him, a good distance away. "And I'm sure you have plenty of tricks up your sleeve." He sniffed. "I know them all."

"Do you?" John leaned back and crossed one leg over the other.

"I know enough not to relax around you." David remained vigilant, gun pointed straight at John. "I am fully aware that you have another weapon tucked in the top of your right boot, so please remove them both." He lifted an eyebrow.

John paused.

"Don't force me to shoot your foot off."

John leaned forward and slid off his right boot, and another gun fell to the floor.

"Kick it over here." David waved the gun again and waited until John did as he was told. "Now, take off the other boot," he instructed.

John did so. "Are you happy?" He raised both hands and waved them in the air.

David shook his head. "I won't be happy until this is over."

"Until what is over?" John seemed genuinely curious. "Are you crossing to the other side? Meeting a Russian agent?"

"Is that what you think?" David huffed. "Is that what they *all* think? Is that why you're here?"

"Well, you have to admit, the situation doesn't look good — you trying to resign, then heading for Russia."

"I wasn't heading for Russia. I headed for Barrow so I could get *here*."

John narrowed his eyes. "Why Barrow? Why here? What in the world could anybody want in Barrow or here? Especially this time of year?"

"I'm meeting someone."

John shook his head. "Exactly as I thought. Meeting someone."

"Not like you think."

"So, like what then?"

"A woman."

"So, you fell in love with a Russian operative? I had you pegged as a little stronger than that."

"No, I fell in love with someone else. Someone from . . . from the future."

John gaped at him. "Are you out of your mind?"

They both stared at each other silently—John obviously trying to size up David's sanity, and David trying to figure out how to explain everything to John.

"No, I'm not out of my mind. Look at yourself, Davidson, then look at me. What do you think is the explanation?"

John shrugged. "Science? They did this on purpose so that I could take care of you."

"Oh, so you just started looking like this recently?"

"Maybe we were twins, separated at birth for some reason." John drummed his fingers on the arm of the couch. "Maybe we're some sort of cousins. Maybe it's just a fluke."

"A fluke?" David raised one eyebrow. "Do you really believe that?"

"Well, what's *your* explanation?"

"In 1967, right here, in this cabin, I met a young woman from the year 2165."

"You've lost your mind, Morse. Don't you think I would have heard about it if something like that had happened?" John began to stand.

"Sit down, John." David waved the gun, and John thumped back down on the couch. "Listen to me, this is important." He leaned forward. "I did something to betray her, so she came back, and we had to live through that time again. Well, *I* had to relive the same experience again, just as it had gone the time before, except the second time, I didn't betray her. All went well save for one thing."

"And that was?" John watched David from under lowered eyelids. He didn't disguise his skepticism.

"In twisting time that way, I was duplicated. She told me that there was someone walking around in this world who had the same DNA as mine. I think we can see *that's* true."

"Ridiculous!" John sat up. "I am not a . . . a . . . copy of you! I was born. I had a mother, and although my father died earlier, I had a father until I was five."

"I had a mother, too, and I, too, had a father until I was five. He died of lung cancer. And yours?"

"This is nonsense." John scowled. "You've obviously looked up my past. You've briefed yourself quite well on my life and even gotten exceptional plastic surgery to look like me." He grabbed the arms of the chair. "I don't know what your game is, but I am not falling for it."

"How could it be a game? Who sent you here? The enemy?"

John looked bemused.

"You were sent by your own people, weren't you?"

John's glare intensified.

"This is real, Davidson." David lifted his shoulders. "Of course, you're a full-fledged human being. We both are, but you existed in some sort of other time continuum and were pulled into this one, I suspect. I don't really understand how all of it works, but because you're here, I can go into Miri's time, and that's where I'm headed. Nothing is going to stop me, not you, not my people, not a storm. Nothing." He clutched the gun so tightly his knuckles turned white.

"Okay, okay, I get it." John raised both hands, palms forward. "Whatever you say, Morse. Relax." He leaned back. "Miri? Is that her name?"

David nodded.

"Pretty. What's she like?"

"Don't." David scowled at him.

"Don't what?"

"Don't make pleasant conversation as if I'm an idiot and don't know what you're doing."

"Well, what exactly do you expect me to do, Morse? You're the one sitting there with a gun pointed at me, telling me some far-fetched story about a girl from the future. It wouldn't be very wise of me to antagonize you, would it?"

"And yet, you do," was David's wry response.

"Perhaps it's that shared DNA," John countered.

David chuckled, so did John.

John tilted his head. "In another world, maybe we could have been friends."

"I seriously doubt it." David's British accent contrasted greatly with John's more informal American. It appeared to be the only difference between them.

"That's true. I'm not a stuck-up Brit."

"It's late." David stood up. "This stuck-up Brit is going to tie you to that solid kitchen chair over there. Then tomorrow, I'm going to meet the woman I love, and you will be free to go wherever you want and live your life away from me."

John rose to his feet and put his hands up. "I'm afraid that's not going to work, Morse. I came here to arrest your contact and to take you back to England. I'm going to have to get my job done."

David shook his head then pushed John toward the kitchen. He threw a rope at John and told him exactly what to do to begin binding himself. Once he felt John was wrapped up enough, David approached and finished the job.

He yawned as he secured the final knot. "I'm sorry you have to sleep like this, John, but it's only for one night."

"I've slept in worse positions."

David nodded. "Yeah, me too." He was surprised at how

exhausted he was from the exchange, but he didn't feel safe going into the bedroom. He decided to sleep out on the couch and keep an eye on things.

CHAPTER THIRTY-THREE: A FLICKER

Once again, David awoke, unsure of what time of day it was. He drew in a sharp gasp, sat up, and checked his watch. He'd be horrified to somehow miss the portal by oversleeping, but he still had plenty of time. It was only 10 a.m. He started to pull himself to his feet.

"Did you have a good night's sleep?" A voice came from the kitchen.

David turned to answer and realized John was sitting there, gun in his lap, untied, and ready to shoot.

"Great." He snarled. "Now what?"

"You'll tell me where you're meeting your connection." John leaned back in the kitchen chair and raised the gun.

David shook his head. "No, you might as well start shooting."

"I could make Swiss cheese out of you." John used the gun to draw a circle in the air.

David shook his head again.

"Okay," John sighed. "I guess you're going to make this difficult." He stood up and walked toward David, keeping his distance. "Your turn to take the kitchen chair. My turn to tie *you* up." He waved David into the kitchen then secured him to the chair. "Now, I need some information." He turned on a burner of the stove, then pulled a knife out of the drawer.

David looked up at John and smirked. "You think I haven't been through worse before? I've had a lot less reason to talk and have put up with a lot more pain. It doesn't matter what you do, I'm not giving you—particularly you—the location of the meeting place. I'll take you with me, but I won't give you the information."

John thrust the knife into the fire on the stove. "I hate to do this to you, buddy, but you leave me no choice." He took the hot knife, then pulled down the front of David's shirt and pressed it against his skin.

David took a deep breath. He squeezed his eyes shut and dug his nails into his palms, but he stayed silent.

"Nothing?" John asked. "I guess you want some more." He thrust the knife back into the flame. "I've done this a million times. I know how to make it hurt."

"And I know how to endure it," David spat out the words.

This time John pushed the hot knife against the back of David's neck. Again, David remained silent. His body tensed, and his eyes closed, but he didn't talk. John continued to work on him, pressing the hot knife against the sensitive skin inside his forearms and on his ankles. Through it all, David continued to withhold the information.

Finally, John backed off. "Okay, have it your way. Take me to her. I'll deal with it when I get there."

David merely nodded.

"What time is the meeting?" John's voice was brusque as he untied David.

"3 p.m." He staggered to his feet, nearly keeling over until he grabbed onto the counter.

John looked at his watch. "We don't have much time, then." He waved the gun. "Get your things."

David slid on his boots and made his way into his coat, every movement causing new agonies where he'd been burned. Once he was dressed, they went out the door. They each drove a snowmobile, John following David's lead, his gun always at the ready.

David knew exactly where the portal was. He had mapped the coordinates out and committed the spot to memory. He drove there with confidence, albeit somewhat weakly after the struggles he'd endured throughout the day. John followed near enough to be intimidating, but he needn't worry. No way David would risk getting shot when he was this close to being with Miri forever.

The place had changed somewhat. The overhang that had been so pronounced three years ago had receded a bit but was still recognizable. David pulled his snowmobile up as close to the entrance as he could, then stopped and dismounted.

John pulled up behind him but remained sitting. "Is this it?"

"Yes."

"Now what?"

"Now, we wait," David answered.

It was nearly three, and it wasn't long before the air began to tingle. David stood up straighter, watching the area near the overhang with expectation.

John climbed off his snowmobile and looked around, eyes darting up and down. "What's going on?" he yelled.

"She's coming from the future," David called back.

John shook his head. "No, what's *really* going on." His voice was wobbly.

David ignored him when Miri's figure shimmered into focus.

"David." She called out to him.

"Miri."

She stepped out of the portal.

John raised his gun. "I'm here to apprehend you in the name of the United States government." He stood straight, his hand trembling just slightly.

"You don't want to do this, Davidson." David turned toward him. "You can see that all I told you was true."

"I don't know." He shook his head. "All I can see is that you're meeting a foreign operative."

"Did that really look like an operative's entrance to you?" David moved to cover Miri. "She will step back into the portal, and I'd like to go with her."

"I'm here to apprehend both of you. You may not leave."

"Are you sure?"

"Yes, I'm sure." John lifted the gun and pointed it.

David raised both hands. "Okay. I'll go back with you, but not her." He stepped forward.

Suddenly, John began to flicker, his hands looking like static in the air. "What's going on?" His voice broke as he looked from one hand to another. He dropped the gun and began to pat his body. "What's happening to me?"

Miri called from behind David. "Because you're forcing David to stay, it appears that you are twisting back into nothing." She stepped out to focus on John. "If you let him go, there will be room for you in this world. The choice is yours."

John's body continued to flicker and fade.

"One of us gets to stay here, Davidson, the other has to go." He reached out toward John. "I have someplace to be. You don't. So what's your decision?"

John's eyes were fading fast, their blue reflecting only snow. His voice could barely be heard when he shouted, "Go!"

Miri grabbed David's hand and pulled him into the portal.

John fell to the ground, then looked down at himself. He was all there. He patted his arms and legs, feeling everything, and he could see everything. He glanced to where Morse and the woman had disappeared, the spot looking as though nothing had happened just moments before. Was this whole encounter just a hallucination?

He shook his head. It was insanity. What had he just seen? Experienced? How would he even report it?

But later, when he called in to discuss it with his superiors, they asked him how his time off had been. They seemed to have no knowledge of any British operative named David Morse. He never existed and, suddenly, John was being credited with dozens of completed missions that he knew he had never done. Jokes about him and some *Belgium Method* were bandied about. He could only infer what that meant and wondered what he would do if called upon to take that sort of action.

Their bodies glowed with the passage of time within swirls of ever-changing colors. On the other side of the time continuum, Miri and David stepped through another portal, hand in hand, and David gasped at what he saw.

The End

ABOUT THE AUTHOR

Luann Lewis is a Chicago native who has spent many years writing legal documents. Now, in semi-retirement, she has recently earned her MFA certification. Dabbling in varied genres, she has had a number of stories, essays, and poems published in print and online as well as had a piece performed professionally as a podcast.